MYSTERY AT MELBECK

Meg Bowering goes to Melbeck House in the Yorkshire Dales to nurse the rich, elderly Mrs Peacock. She likes her patient and is immediately attracted to Mrs Peacock's nephew and heir, Geoffrey, who farms nearby. But Geoffrey is a gambling man and Meg could never have foreseen the dreadful chain of events which follow. Throughout her ordeal, she is helped by the local vicar, Andrew Sheratt, and she soon discovers where her heart really lies.

GILLIAN KAYE

◆

MYSTERY AT MELBECK

Complete and Unabridged

LINFORD
Leicester

First published in Great Britain

First Linford Edition
published 1999

British Library CIP Data

Kaye, Gillian
    Mystery at Melbeck.—Large print ed.—
Linford romance library
    1. Love stories
    2. Large type books
    I. Title
    823.9'14 [F]

    ISBN 0–7089–5510–X

Published by
F. A. Thorpe (Publishing) Ltd.
Anstey, Leicestershire

Set by Words & Graphics Ltd.
Anstey, Leicestershire
Printed and bound in Great Britain by
T. J. International Ltd., Padstow, Cornwall

This book is printed on acid-free paper

1

Meg got back into her car which was parked outside the post office in the small market town of Hexton, trying to remember the directions she had been given for getting to Melbeck House in Wedderdale. She was to go up the dale as far as Nether Rawcliffe, take the turning by the pottery then keep on up the hill until she reached the farm. Mrs Manthorpe at the farm would tell her how to reach the house.

As she put her key in the ignition, she smiled at the friendly curiosity of the lady in the post office, it was obvious that she was coming to an area where everyone knew everybody else.

Meg was Margaret Anne Bowering but could not remember ever being called anything else but Meg. She was twenty-five and for the past four years had been working as a nurse in a big Leeds hospital; she had been very happy there but after weeks of working nights plus splitting up with her boyfriend, Bruce, she was feeling very tired and dispirited. She felt as though she needed a change and before long she had seen an advertisement in the Yorkshire Post for a nurse to look after an elderly lady in Wedderdale.

Suddenly, the prospect of doing private nursing appealed to her though she knew from her friends' experiences that it could be very difficult; but that wasn't the only appeal. After four years of city life and working in a large hospital, the thought of a remote dale seemed like bliss. She had applied, made the arrangements with Mrs Peacock of Melbeck House over the phone and now she was on her way.

After driving for a while, following the instructions she'd been given, she managed to find the farm she'd been looking for. Parking the car, she walked quickly up the short path to a solid oak door and knocked rather tentatively. Before long, the door was opened and she stood staring into the eyes of one of the most good-looking men she had ever seen. He was very tall, his hair was raven black and the grey eyes in the handsome face were at the same time smiling and questioning.

Meg felt flustered and was annoyed with herself.

'I was told to ask for Mrs Manthorpe. Are you Mr Manthorpe?'

His reaction did nothing to reassure her; he roared with laughter.

'No, I'm not Mr Manthorpe, but come in, come in. It is not often we have a beautiful girl visiting High Aiskew.'

'I won't come in. I am looking for Melbeck House and the lady in the post office at Hexton told me to stop at High Aiskew farm and ask for directions.'

He smiled and stepped outside the door looking down at her with increasing interest.

'If you're looking for Melbeck House then you must be the new nurse my aunt is expecting.'

'Your aunt . . . ' Meg stammered.

'Yes, I'm Geoffrey Peacock and I manage the farm for her. Aunt Ethel isn't very well and doesn't seem to be able to find a nurse who will stay. I must say you are an improvement on the last couple we had. Are you sure you want to work up here in the middle of nowhere?'

She didn't like his jokey manner but he was being quite friendly and it was beginning to look as though she would have to deal with him as well as with Mrs Peacock.

'I think I do,' she replied. 'I've been working in Leeds for four years and it seemed like a good opportunity to have a complete change.'

'Well, I hope you're right. Aunt Ethel isn't a difficult person and I shall certainly come to see her more often if I know I am going to find you there.'

Meg was silent but her heart was sinking; were there going to be hidden problems before she had even started?

'I'd be glad if you would show me the way to the house,' she said.

'Come down to the gate.'

She followed him as he walked away from the house.

'That's Melbeck House,' he told her, pointing up the narrow lane to a distant clump of trees sheltering a square, stone house. 'And above is Melbeck Moor. I must take you up there one day. Do you ride?'

She shook her head. 'No, I don't,' she said shortly. 'Thank you, I'll be on my way.'

He was smiling again. 'Don't rush off, I don't even know your name.'

'It's Meg Bowering.'

'Meg, good. I shall look forward to seeing you again, Meg. Give my love to Aunt Ethel and tell her I'll be up as usual on Friday afternoon.'

Meg drove off, her mind in a whirl; complications before she had even reached the house. Geoffrey Peacock was certainly attractive and she wondered if he was married. She thought he must have been in his early thirties.

She soon found herself in front of the large, stone house and as she got out of the car, the front door was opening before she had time to knock and a smiling lady stood there, she was short and plump with grey hair permed into tight curls.

'Hello, I heard the car,' she was saying as she held the door open. 'You must be Nurse Bowering, we've been expecting you. I hope you didn't have trouble finding us, it's rather out of the way. Oh, I must introduce myself. I'm Mrs Coates — Mrs Peacock's housekeeper. Welcome to Melbeck House.'

Meg shook hands with Mrs Coates and felt a sense of relief at the kind welcome.

'Hello, yes, I'm Meg,' she said. 'I found my way here quite easily. I met

Mr Peacock at the farm and he gave me directions.'

The housekeeper frowned.

'So you've met Geoffrey, have you? That means he'll soon be paying us a visit. However, you'll be hearing enough about Geoffrey Peacock. Come and meet Mrs Peacock. We'll bring your luggage in later.'

Meg was looking around her and liked what she saw. A square entrance hall with thick carpet, wide staircase and a solid oak chest on which stood a lovely bowl of daffodils just coming into flower.

She followed Mrs Coates into a large room at the front of the house; it felt warm and welcoming with a cheerful, log fire burning in the grate and in a wheel-chair by the side of the fireplace was a small lady with a bright face and beautiful white hair.

'Here's Nurse Bowering, ma'am,' Mrs Coates said and Meg found her hand held in a surprisingly firm grasp.

7

'I can't get up to welcome you, Nurse Bowering. You will soon learn that I find it difficult to stand. But you are very welcome and I hope we shall get on well together. Now I believe your name is Margaret. I think it suits you very well.'

Meg found herself liking the old lady immediately.

'I'm usually called Meg,' she said.

'No, I don't believe in shortening names. I shall stick to Margaret. Now sit down and tell me something about yourself. Did I hear you say to Mrs Coates that you've already met my scapegrace of a nephew?'

'Yes, when I called at the farm to ask the way to Melbeck House.'

'Nice enough chap but not really given to hard work — prefers to go off riding or to the races. Tell me,' she said, changing the subject, 'do you have a boyfriend?'

Meg was startled but amused. Mrs Peacock was obviously quite a character and you couldn't help wondering what she was going to say next.

'No, I haven't got a boyfriend. I did have but we split up.'

Mrs Peacock looked at her with a compelling glance.

'Well, don't go falling for my nephew. All the young ones do. He knows how to get round them. I'm warning you not to take him seriously. I don't want you to get upset. I think I'm going to like you and I don't want you breaking your heart over Geoffrey.

'He's only ever looked at one woman seriously and that's Carla Handley from the village. Older than he is but very attractive and seems to have some hold over him. I'm surprised that they haven't married years ago but I did hear that she cannot have children and he knows that I want a Peacock heir. But she may catch him yet, and she knows he's worth a million when I'm gone.'

'Mrs Peacock,' Meg started to protest.

'Oh, you'll get used to my plain speaking. I know I'm getting on for eighty and I've got this arthritis but

I'm strong and I've got a good doctor. I'll make Geoffrey wait a few years yet.' She gave a short laugh.

'Now, I've shocked you. I'll stop talking and let Mrs Coates show you to your room. I hope you like it — I've spared no expense for my nurses. They've got to be comfortable living right up here. Ring that bell, my dear, and Mrs Coates will come.'

Meg was taken up the stairs and noticed with relief that there was a stair lift; she was soon to realise what Mrs Peacock had meant when she had said she spared no expense. She was shown into a large room facing west with a glorious view right across the dale. It was furnished as a bed-sitting room with comfortable furniture and its own bathroom; there was a television set, a table with an electric kettle and everything for making tea or coffee and she would have her own phone.

She turned to Mrs Coates.

'It's absolute luxury after my bed-sit in Leeds. How kind Mrs Peacock is.' She stopped and looked at the older woman. 'Does she always talk like that?'

Mrs Coates gave a merry laugh.

'She's a dear and I could tell that she's taken to you. She's like that on her good days but if she has a bad day and is in a lot of pain you'll find that she's very quiet but she never complains.'

'Only about her nephew.' Meg let the words slip out.

'I'm afraid so. He's a great disappointment to her. Always looking for money to pay his gambling debts. She would like to see him married and settled down with children at the farm but I don't know that it will ever come to that. He's a dark horse and no mistake.'

Meg was to settle into life at Melbeck House very quickly and felt somehow ashamed that the work was so easy. She found she had plenty of free time and Mrs Peacock had encouraged her to go out as often as possible.

'Now, Margaret,' she said. 'Try to get out and see some of the countryside when you have time off. Melbeck Moor is worth the climb and on a clear day you can see as far as the Lake District.'

So that's what Meg decided to do — it was better than sitting in the house watching the television on her days off. Climbing the moor wasn't easy at first but after days of perseverance she found she could manage it in half an hour.

Mrs Peacock had been right about the view and far in the distance she could see the peaks of Cumbria which she told herself she would visit one day. When she got back to the house and changed back into her uniform, Mrs Peacock loved to have tea with her and hear about her trips.

'I've walked up there ever since I was first married,' she would say. 'William, my husband, was always busy on the farm so I went on my own. Then after he died and we had no son to carry on the farm, I was glad for Geoffrey to come and take over and we bought Melbeck House for me to live in. I didn't want to be under Geoffrey's feet and I like it up here. So the arrangement worked out quite well.'

It didn't take long for Geoffrey Peacock to learn what Meg's movements were in the afternoons. He was always at Melbeck House on a Friday afternoon when he had tea with his aunt and gave her his report. At other times he would turn up unexpectedly, much to Meg's annoyance.

One particularly sunny day when she had been at Melbeck for a couple of weeks, she was enjoying her usual walk to the top of the moor. Having climbed steadily and reached the top, she heard the sound of horse's hooves coming ever closer.

Within a couple of minutes she realised it was Geoffrey Peacock and she couldn't help feeling a bit annoyed at having her precious privacy invaded.

'Hello, Meg. Aunt Ethel told me you came up here sometimes, so I thought

I'd come and find you.'

'I was enjoying being on my own actually,' she replied rather stiffly, secretly feeling a bit flustered.

'That's not very friendly. Everyone needs a bit of company sometimes, and not just from Aunt Ethel and Mrs Coates.'

'Your aunt is a dear,' she said. 'And she's very good to me. I get plenty of free time to do what I want.'

He had perched himself on the rock beside her and was looking at her quite seriously.

'Do you think she's keeping well? Sometimes I see her and I'm not too sure.'

She looked at him, shocked.

'Apart from her bad arthritis she's actually very healthy and could live for years yet.'

She suddenly felt his hand grasp her arm quite fiercely and she looked up startled; she saw a deeply worried frown on his face, a dark look in his eyes.

'But I've always thought . . . I mean, if she needs a nurse it must mean that she is quite ill.'

'To be honest, it's not really a nurse she needs. It's just someone to help her dress and bath and get up and down stairs. I love being here and I know I have to be on call at night but you wouldn't have to be a nurse to do the job properly. I would think she's got ten years in her at least.'

'You're not serious, are you?'

'What's the matter?' Meg was puzzled. 'I thought you would be pleased to know that she was not as bad as you had imagined.'

The frown was still there and Meg found it impossible to tell what he was thinking; she had spoken truthfully but what she had said seemed to have thrown him into confusion.

'Of course I'm pleased,' he blustered. 'It's very good news — couldn't be better news, in fact.'

Meg didn't think he sounded very sincere but she didn't reply and got up ready to walk back down to the house.

'Don't go, Meg, not yet. I want to get to know you. Tell me something about yourself.'

She shook off the hand he had placed on her arm and moved away from him.

'No, I must get back,' she said. 'I always have tea with Mrs Peacock at four o'clock.'

'Well, if you have to go,' he said lightly. 'When's your day off, Meg?'

'Either Saturday or Sunday. Mrs Coates and I take it in turns.'

'Maybe I could take you out some time — we could go over to Wharfedale or have a trip to Harrogate if you would like that.'

'Mr Peacock . . . '

'Please, call me Geoffrey — it's a lot less formal.'

'Well then, Geoffrey,' Meg said, smiling, 'I'll have to see. I'm not sure what I'll be doing with my week-ends yet.'

He started to put his riding hat on and she felt glad she wasn't going to have to make more excuses. He touched her lightly on the shoulder.

'I'll see you on Friday, then you can let me know. Goodbye.'

Meg watched him disappear into the distance. There was no doubt he was extremely attractive but there was something about his manner she didn't quite like.

When Friday came, Mrs Peacock wasn't having a very good day. Although Meg wanted to stay with her, Mrs Peacock was drowsy from the pain-killers so Meg decided to go out for a walk instead.

It was a breezy, showery day more like April than May and Meg walked quickly thinking that she would just go along the path above the farm rather than go to the top of the moor. She was wearing an old pair of jeans and a cotton shirt and when a heavy shower came she was quickly soaked and decided to turn back.

She went in the back door of the house and straight up to her room to change into her uniform; it was not quite tea-time but she decided to go to see if Mrs Peacock had woken yet.

As she ran down the stairs, she was startled by the sound of raised voices coming from the living-room. It soon became obvious that Geoffrey and his aunt were having quite a heated argument about something.

'Geoffrey, it's not the first time that I've told you that I'm not going to advance you any of the money. You are a spendthrift and a gambler and however much I gave you, it would all be spent at the race-course. I'll not have it.'

'Aunt Ethel, it's quite stupid to have all that money tied up in shares when we need capital to improve the farm. You seem to think that I spend my life on a race-course — well, it's not true. The farm needs the money.' His voice was raised and angry and Meg could hear him clearly.

'The farm is doing very well and you know it; it has always done well. Your uncle and his father before him worked hard all their lives and the farm prospered. It is still prospering and you make quite enough to put back into it to keep it modernised without needing to touch any of my money. I'll not have good money going after bad and that's my final word on the subject.'

'You're an obstinate, old woman.' Geoffrey raised his voice even more and there was a nasty note to it. 'You pretend you're ill and not going to last long and now I hear you'll probably go on for years. You're so incredibly unreasonable . . .'

Mrs Peacock's voice sounded faint but Meg just caught what she was saying.

'That's quite enough, Geoffrey. Will you please find Meg. I'm not feeling well . . .'

But Meg had heard enough. She opened the door quickly and collided

19

with Geoffrey who was on his way out.

'You were listening, you little busybody. It's all your fault. You'd better see to her.'

Meg took no notice of his words, and was alarmed to see Mrs Peacock slumped back in her chair, her face ashen grey. Quickly, Meg took her pulse just as Mrs Peacock began to come round.

'Meg, thank goodness you're here. I can't really remember what happened . . .'

'It's all right — you fainted, Mrs Peacock.' Meg patted the old woman's hand. 'But you're going to be fine.'

'And Geoffrey? What about Geoffrey?' Mrs Peacock began to panic and Meg tried to calm her down. 'Don't worry about him. He's already left. I don't think he was too happy after the argument you had but I'm sure things will be all right in the end.'

Mrs Peacock was shaking her head. 'No, Meg. I don't think so. You don't know what Geoffrey's like.'

'I think I have a good idea. Your argument with him was quite loud. I'm afraid I overheard quite a bit of what was going on.'

2

Mrs Peacock opened her eyes wide. 'Meg you are a good girl but you shouldn't listen at doors,' she said.

Meg managed a smile. She had noticed that at last her employer had dropped the hated Margaret.

'I'm sorry, Mrs Peacock, I was coming down to see you when I got back from my walk and I could hear shouting and I didn't know what to do, so somehow I just stayed there.'

'In that case, you know what it was all about, what Geoffrey said to me?'

'Yes, and both of you sounded angry — especially Geoffrey.'

'There's a lot of bad temper under all that good-looking charm. He got it from my brother-in-law. But then he was an only son and allowed to have his own way. When his parents died there wasn't a lot of money so he was glad enough when I offered him the farm. He had never settled himself in a career but just drifted from one job to another when he wasn't at home living off his parents. And, of course, he knows it will all be his one day.

'He's not like William, I'm afraid. I wish he was. We wouldn't have all the problems about the money.' She was silent for a moment, back in the past, then she looked pointedly at Meg. 'Do you think I am in the wrong, Meg? Perhaps I should just give him the money to do what he wants with it.'

Meg was surprised at being asked her opinion.

'Mrs Peacock, it really is none of my business. Only you can decide what is best for you and Geoffrey. I'm just concerned that you are going to make yourself more ill if you go on having that kind of argument.'

'I'll be careful, Meg dear, and I don't think it will happen again. Geoffrey knows me too well and if he presses me too hard, he knows that I'm capable of changing my will and leaving the money and the farm to some family I have in Ireland.'

'I haven't heard about them before,' Meg said quickly, keen to change the subject.

She was rewarded with a smile.

'They're only distant family, I know, but I still like to keep in touch. They're from my mother's side and are my second cousins but I do feel like more of an aunt to them. I always intended to give them something anyway, but Geoffrey knows if he pushes me too far they'll get everything and he won't get a penny.'

Meg was glad to see Mrs Peacock more like her old self again.

'Come on, I think we'll get you to bed early tonight,' she said. 'You've had enough for one day.'

'Yes, I think you're right. And the vicar's coming over in the morning so I want to be up in good time.'

Next morning, while they were waiting for the vicar to arrive, Mrs

Peacock told Meg a little about him.

'He's a nice young man — in his early thirties, I think. His name is Andrew Sheratt and he's unmarried which I think is a pity in a vicar. I have hopes of him and Jill Burnett, the infant teacher at the school in Nether Rawcliffe. She's a sweetie, runs the church Youth Club and I think she gets on very well with Andrew. I keep hoping they'll announce their engagement but if they are seeing one another, they keep very quiet about it!'

Mrs Peacock was thoughtful for a moment and Meg wondered what she was going to come out with next.

'On the other hand, Jill's name is also often linked with David Courtney who is the head-teacher of the school. He is a good man but has great sadness in his life as his wife died just a year ago. He's bringing up their two little girls on his own. I think Jill helps him sometimes at the week-ends but I don't think there is a romance there.

It's too soon. She would be better off with Andrew.'

Meg laughed.

'Mrs Peacock, you are match-making.'

'And why not! We all like a romance and I've a great wish to see Andrew happily married. He works hard with four parishes in his care and he is very well-liked. He needs a wife. I think he is very attractive in a quiet way. See what you think when we comes, Meg. I haven't asked you if you are a churchgoer.'

Meg shook her head.

'I used to go when I was younger but I got out of the habit when I was at the hospital. Perhaps it would be a good idea to start going again now that I'm going to be part of a village community.'

When Andrew Sheratt did come, Meg was to get a surprise and to experience feelings she thought she had put behind her when she had split up with Bruce. Mrs Coates brought him into the living-room. He shook hands with Mrs Peacock and then turned to Meg as Mrs Peacock introduced them.

'Andrew, this is Margaret Bowering who likes to be called Meg. Meg, meet Andrew, vicar of Nether Rawcliffe, Linford Bridge, Upper Rawcliffe and Wedder Head. Doesn't that sound impressive?'

They all laughed, which broke the ice. Meg found herself shaking a firm hand and looking into brown smiling eyes. Andrew Sheratt was of medium height but much taller than Meg. He had rather untidy light-brown hair which gave him a boyish appearance and his even features were young and unlined.

As their eyes met, there was a sudden current of feeling between them which gave Meg quite a jolt. As she felt his fingers firm about hers, Meg's heart was fluttering and she was saying to herself, I could fall for Andrew Sheratt but I must be careful. He is someone else's property, according to Mrs Peacock.

'How are you liking it in Wedderdale?' he was asking her.

Meg had no hesitation.

'It is beautiful,' she replied. 'And we are wonderfully situated here with Melbeck Moor on our doorstep.'

'You've discovered the moor, then?'

'Yes, and I go up there whenever I can.'

'I don't have much time for walking,' he said seriously. 'But one of my favourite places is at the top of the dale at Wedder Head.'

'Is that one of your churches?'

'Yes, it's the smallest but it's something special. It commands a view right down the dale. You must go there if you can.'

Meg would have liked to have gone on talking to him but he had come to see Mrs Peacock so she made her excuses and left them on their own. After half an hour, she heard him at the front door and went to see him out. As he smiled at her, her heart nearly turned over.

'Come out to the gate with me. I have something to ask you,' he said quietly.

She stood at the gate and looked up at him wondering what he was going to say.

'Mrs Peacock tells me you were once a church-goer and I wondered if you were thinking of joining as at Nether Rawcliffe.'

'I haven't really thought about it,' she replied honestly.

'Well, I'm not trying to coerce you into coming but the truth is we need someone to help with the Youth Club. It's run by Jill Burnett, the infant teacher at the village school. She started up the club about a year ago because there was nothing in the village for the young people and it has been a great success. The thing is, Jill could really do with some help and as soon as I saw you, I thought you might be the person to ask. You are about the same age as Jill and I think you would get on well together. What do you think, or am I rushing you?'

The last words were said with a smile, but Meg's mind was racing. It would be nice to be involved in village life and not always confined to the two elderly ladies at Melbeck House.

'It really depends if I can get Mrs Peacock ready for bed before the Youth Club starts. I'd like to help very much but I've got to put my duties here first.'

'I understand that,' he replied. 'Why don't you go down and see Jill at the school one afternoon? The children go home at three-thirty. Can I tell her you'll go and see her?'

Meg had no resistance against his persuasive friendliness and she liked the idea.

'Well, yes, I'd like to go and see her. It's the one thing I've missed up here, meeting people of my own age.'

'Well, here's your chance!'

He grinned and held out his hand. When she put hers into it, he didn't let go for a minute.

'And, Meg, perhaps you would let me show you Wedder Head one day. Would you let me take you up there?'

Meg felt she was on dangerous ground. She would have liked to have said yes but she was remembering what Mrs Peacock had said about Andrew and Jill Burnett, she didn't want to cause any trouble there.

'I'll see,' she said. 'I don't have a lot of free time, just an hour in the afternoon. I'm not grumbling, for I love looking after Mrs Peacock but I'm not in a position to make any promises.'

'Fair enough, I won't rush you. We'll see how it goes and I'll tell Jill that you'll pop down to the school to see her one afternoon.'

Meg was thoughtful as she watched his car disappearing in the direction of the farm. Meeting someone like Andrew Sheratt had been totally unexpected and she found herself wishing that she could take up his offer of going to Webber Head. But all thoughts of Andrew were banished from her mind that afternoon with the appearance of a much changed Geoffrey, just as Mrs Peacock had said.

Meg was coming through the field on her way back from the moor when she saw someone opening the gate at the bottom of the garden. Geoffrey's height and his striking black hair were unmissable and Meg felt uncomfortable remembering his last words to her.

'Meg,' he called out as he walked towards her, 'Aunt Ethel is asleep and I didn't want to disturb her so I thought I'd come and look for you. I want to talk to you.'

She could hardly believe that it was the same man who had raised his voice in anger the previous day. He was now all smiles and took her arm gently to guide her through the gate and to a wooden seat under the trees at the bottom of the garden. She didn't say anything to him until they were sitting down, afraid of losing her temper and starting an argument with him.

'I don't think I want to speak to you

after yesterday's performance,' she said very quietly.

'Meg, you'll have to forgive me and so will Aunt Ethel. I know I've got an awful temper but you mustn't read too much into what I say in the heat of the moment.'

She looked up at him. He was serious and in earnest and she knew she would have to give him the benefit of the doubt.

'I don't care what you say to me,' she said. 'It's Mrs Peacock who is my concern. I don't like to see her getting upset like that.'

He took her hand and held it tightly though she tried to pull away.

'I'm sorry, Meg, I really am. To be quite honest, I've got into a mess financially and it would be so easy for Aunt Ethel to help me out. She's loaded and it's all coming to me one day in any case.'

She did pull her hand away this time and was goaded into replying rather hotly.

'I wouldn't be too sure of that, Geoffrey.'

He laughed out loud.

'She's been telling you about the Irish cousins. It's her little ploy to try to get me to stop gambling. She'll never leave the farm away from the Peacocks. Most of the money was Uncle William's and there have been Peacocks farming here for generations. It was certainly a Peacock ancestor who built the farmhouse at High Aiskew in the first place.'

'But there isn't another generation to pass it on to,' Meg said.

'There will be, Meg, there will be. I'm only thirty-four. There's plenty of time. I've been waiting for someone pretty and appealing, like you, to come along.'

Meg was cross and she showed it.

'That's enough of that kind of talk, Geoffrey Peacock. I'm going in to see if Mrs Peacock is awake yet.'

She stood up and found him towering closely over her, his hands on her

34

shoulders. She twisted away but he bent his head and kissed her. It was a brief embrace but it surprised Meg and she was startled at her response to the feel of his lips. She was horrified to realise that she had almost felt that she wanted the kiss to continue and she knew that she must guard against the attraction of this man.

'Meg,' he was whispering, 'you didn't mind me kissing you.'

'I did mind,' she returned sharply. 'I want no kisses from a man who can speak to an old lady as you spoke to Mrs Peacock yesterday. I'm not staying with you a minute longer.'

And, turning, she didn't give him a backward glance as she walked quickly back to the house while Geoffrey watched her with some amusement. She was a pretty, little thing, he was thinking, and with some character. Maybe just the type of girl who would make him a good wife and give him an heir to High Aiskew and thus to the Peacock fortune. Rather smugly, he followed her into Melbeck House.

Meg didn't hear his interview with his aunt but he must have turned on his charm and said something to make Mrs Peacock smile and feel happier, and he left with a cheque in his pocket and a joking word to Meg at the front door.

'Meg, all is well, thanks to you. I think I'll be popping in more often in the future.'

Meg had no idea what he could mean but said goodbye and shut the door on him. She hurried to the living-room to see how Mrs Peacock was.

'Meg, there you are. I told you he would come and apologise. I still refuse to part with the money to settle his gambling debts but he has given me hope that there still might be a future generation of Peacocks at High Aiskew. Do you like him, Meg?'

Meg looked up startled. What on earth had Geoffrey said to his aunt to prompt such a question?

'No, I don't like him at all,' she

replied. 'I'm sorry, Mrs Peacock, I know that he's your nephew but I think he's an unprincipled charmer and I wouldn't trust him for a minute.'

Mrs Peacock laughed.

'I know all that,' she said, 'But he's a Peacock and he'll make someone a good husband one day. Let's have some tea, Meg, I feel a lot better than I did yesterday.'

★ ★ ★

Meg didn't forget her promise to Andrew that she would go and see Jill Burnett and when they did meet, she liked Jill immediately.

She took the car down to the village one afternoon and parked outside the school. It was a compact, Victorian building and was a large school for the size of the village. It did, in fact, serve all the farms and villages for miles around and the children were brought in by bus. Meg made her way round to the back, following the mothers when

37

the time drew near for the children to come out.

A tall, slim girl with dark hair was standing at the door seeing the children off and with her stood a burly man with slightly greying hair. When most of the children had gone, Meg went up and introduced herself and straight away received a welcoming smile.

'Oh, I'm so pleased to meet you. I'm Jill Burnett and this is David Courtney, our head teacher.'

Meg shook hands with them both and was invited into the school. Jill busied herself with the last of the children while Meg had a word with David Courtney.

'You've got quite a big school here,' she said.

'Yes. We serve the whole dale and we've got four classes in the junior school. Each class is small so the children are very fortunate. Some of them come from quite remote farms so they have a long way to travel. Are you the person who has offered to help with the Youth Club, by the way?'

Meg smiled.

'Well, I'm not sure if I'll be of any use yet.'

'Jill has done very well to build it up as she has done. It's a credit to her, but she's desperate for help. We've started to get youngsters in from the other villages and we don't want to turn them away. Here she is now. I'll leave you to talk it over with her.'

Jill took Meg into the now quiet school-room.

'Andrew told me that you might come,' she said. 'Would you really be willing to help with the club?'

'I'm quite willing but it really depends what time it starts and if I can fit it in with my duties.'

Jill looked interested.

'You're with old Mrs Peacock up at Melbeck House, aren't you? Look, I've got a lot of clearing up to do now. What about coming to my place one evening for a coffee and we'll talk about it?'

Meg nodded.

'Yes, that would be fine. Would you like me to come back down later this evening?'

'Could you? I live at Greystones, the little cottage next to the post office. Do you know where I mean?'

'Yes, I think so. Would eight o'clock be all right? I'll have settled Mrs Peacock by then.'

'Yes, that's great, I'll see you later then.'

The two of them got on really well that evening. They discovered that they were the same age and both of them had lived in Leeds. Jill eagerly told Meg about the Youth Club and what she was trying to do.

'They really are a super bunch of kids but they do like to be doing something with a purpose. They are quite happy to play table tennis or darts or to have some disco dancing for part of the evening but I like to have something interesting to offer them. Last winter, we did local and family history and they loved that. Now that's completed and I've got to think of something for next winter. Summer is all right as we go on rambles or bird-watching or something like that. Have you got any bright ideas?'

'I don't think I'm going to be of any use. The only thing I know anything about is nursing. I don't suppose a first aid course would be any good, would it?'

Jill's face lit up instantly.

'First aid! That's brilliant. They'll be really keen and it's very important, too. Oh, I could hug you.'

Meg laughed.

'Hold on! It would take two of us. Have you done any first aid?'

Jill shook her head.

'No, but you could teach me over the summer and we could start the class after the holidays. Would you be willing to do that?'

'Yes, I think so. Have we got any funds for equipment and things?'

'Oh, yes, the villagers are really good.

People are keen for the children to have somewhere to go and all sorts of events are going on to raise money for the club. We are very lucky and . . . '

She stopped speaking as she heard a knock on the door.

'Oh, that'll be Andrew. I told him you were coming tonight.'

Meg felt a sinking of the heart. She had met him briefly after church on Sunday and felt the same tug of his personality but it looked as though Mrs Peacock had been right when she had linked his name with Jill Burnett's. But she soon put all thoughts of the attraction of Andrew Sheratt from her mind as the three of them sat and chatted over coffee.

They had a lot to discuss and later, as Meg drove home, she admitted that she'd had a very pleasant evening. She might have to accept that Andrew belonged to Jill but at least it looked as though she would have them both as good friends.

3

The days sped by and spring quickly turned to summer. Meg was happy at Melbeck House except for one thing. Geoffrey had been true to his word and they saw him more often. He would join her on the top of the moor and she felt her solitary hour quite spoiled. He would also appear for coffee in the morning and he badgered her into letting him take her out. She would never accept. He was good company but she could not take to him.

What was even worse was that Mrs Peacock seemed to encourage the relationship and Meg began to wonder if, in fact, Geoffrey had hinted to her that he would find Meg acceptable as a wife. His former companion, Carla Handley, the rich widow who lived in the village, was never mentioned. Meg had never met her and Mrs Peacock had ceased to talk about her.

In the end, Meg was forced into Geoffrey's company through no fault of her own. Mrs Peacock had to visit Leeds for an X-ray and to see her consultant rheumatologist and Geoffrey decided that it would make more sense to take her in his Range Rover than to try and get her and the wheelchair into Meg's small car.

The day went well. It was one of Mrs Peacock's better days and Meg thought that her patient was looking forward to the trip just as a change from being confined to Melbeck House. Geoffrey was all kindness and consideration and showed a lot of patience with his aunt.

By the time they got home, Meg had even begun to wonder if she had misjudged him. Mrs Peacock was very pleased with herself as the X-ray showed no deterioration in her condition and the consultant was optimistic that the drugs he was giving her were helping to slow up the progress of her complaint. As Geoffrey wheeled his aunt back into Melbeck House, Mrs Peacock thanked him.

'Geoffrey, you have been very good and I have enjoyed my day out even if it was to visit the hospital. Couldn't the three of us do it again? We could find a nice place to visit and have a picnic or something. We've got the whole of the summer in front of us.'

And so the following week found Meg sitting in the car with Geoffrey and Mrs Peacock on the way to visit Bolton Abbey. Meg enjoyed the day. Geoffrey couldn't have been nicer and Mrs Peacock was delighted. They finished the day in the restaurant of the abbey and Mrs Peacock insisted that she would sit there quietly while Geoffrey took Meg for a walk.

Meg could see that nothing could have pleased Geoffrey more and as she was feeling well-disposed towards him because of his kindness to his aunt, she agreed to go. The path along the river was quiet. They crossed the bridge and walked slowly through the trees on the other side. Geoffrey had taken her by the hand and while Meg did not wish to give him any encouragement, it has seemed no more than a friendly gesture and she did not protest.

Meg hadn't forgotten her original dislike of Geoffrey or his outrageous behaviour but he seemed so changed that it was almost as though she was with a different person. It had been a pleasant day and she wasn't prepared to spoil it. She hoped that Geoffrey wouldn't do or say anything to upset her.

They came to a part where the path left the edge of the water and went steeply up through the trees. Geoffrey pulled at her hand as she lagged behind and he laughed at her.

'Meg, I thought you were getting fit walking up to the moor every day and here you are, puffing and panting.'

Meg laughed, too.

'It's your fault! You're going too

quickly for me and I can't keep up with you.'

He slowed down instantly and tightened his hold on her hand.

'I'm sorry. Let's go back and sit on the stones by the water.'

'We mustn't be too long. I didn't really like leaving Mrs Peacock on her own.'

'If I know Aunt Ethel, she'll have found someone to talk to. She has enjoyed her day, hasn't she? And have you, Meg? Don't you think we're getting on rather well?'

'Is that supposed to mean anything?' she replied rather waspishly.

'No, not really. It's just that I find I like being with you very much and my thoughts always seem to veer towards the future.'

'It needn't be a future that includes me,' she said.

'Ah, I may make you change your mind yet and today has been a step in the right direction.'

He put his arm round her shoulders

and pulled her towards him, reaching for her lips. But Meg stood up abruptly.

'Today has been a day for bringing Mrs Peacock to Bolton Abbey and that's all there is to it. It's time we were getting back,' she said abruptly.

Geoffrey didn't argue and they walked quickly back to find Mrs Peacock quite happily talking to a couple.

Two days later, Meg was to have a surprise visitor at Melbeck House. It was mid-morning, she had settled Mrs Peacock in the living-room and was up in her bedroom tidying up. Following a tap on her door, she heard Mrs Coates' voice.

'There's a visitor for you, Miss Meg, down in the living-room.'

For a second, Meg's heart jumped. Could it possibly be Andrew? Then she chided herself for being foolish and hurried downstairs. She could hear voices coming from the living-room but it was not a male voice. As she went in, she was surprised to see Mrs Peacock talking to a tall, rather good-looking but haughty woman of about forty. She was very well-dressed, with a lot of jewellery and hair immaculately groomed. She turned as Meg entered the room.

'Meg,' Mrs Peacock said, 'this is Carla Handley. You've heard me speak of her. She is a friend of Geoffrey's.'

Meg felt herself dwarfed by the older woman but she shook hands politely.

'I've come on rather a private matter,' Carla said.

Meg felt mystified and not sure of what to do.

'Would you like to come up to my room? I'll make us some coffee.'

She looked at her employer.

'Is that all right, Mrs Peacock?'

'Yes, of course, but come and see me again before you go, Carla.'

Meg took her visitor upstairs and sat her in the one easy chair while she made some coffee. Then, seated, she looked at Carla wondering why she should be seeking her out. It didn't take long to find out.

'Meg — you don't mind if I call you Meg — I have come to say something very particular to you. We have never met before but I have heard a lot about you through different people in the village. I want to know what is going on between you and Geoffrey Peacock.'

Meg was taken aback. She knew that Geoffrey's name was linked with Carla's and she had heard both Geoffrey and Mrs Peacock speak of her. Carla didn't wait for a reply.

'I've heard of your meetings on the moor, and I know that Geoffrey is to be seen more frequently at Melbeck House. I also know that I have seen very little of him during the last few weeks. Now I believe you've taken to going out for the day with him.'

Meg interrupted suddenly and could hardly keep her temper.

'Mrs Handley . . . '

'No, please call me Carla. I've no

wish to be unfriendly.'

Meg nearly laughed aloud. There hadn't been a lot of friendliness in Carla's words so far.

'If Geoffrey chooses to come to see his aunt more often, it's nothing to do with me. As for meeting on the moor — I can only tell you that I go often for a quiet walk in the afternoon and my enjoyment of the peace and quiet is spoiled by his appearances. As for going out for the day with him, that is quite true but the first time was to take Mrs Peacock to hospital and the second time, a few days ago, was because she wanted to go to Bolton Abbey. I thought it wiser to be with her.'

Carla was curiously silent, frowning a little.

'Don't you like Geoffrey? Haven't you fallen for him?'

Meg decided that only forthrightness would do with this woman.

'Geoffrey Peacock knows how to turn on the charm but it doesn't make me like him. He has been very kind to Mrs

Peacock on the two occasions we have been out and I respect him for that but I certainly haven't fallen for him. Does that satisfy you?'

Carla gave the glimmer of a smile.

'You are very outspoken but I am pleased. I had heard your name coupled with Geoffrey's and I came to tell you that it is my intention to marry Geoffrey Peacock myself.'

Meg found herself wondering if Geoffrey knew anything of this intention but she remained polite.

'Then I have to congratulate you. Mrs Peacock has often said that she wished Geoffrey would get married.'

'But if Mrs Peacock hopes to see another generation of the family at High Aiskew then she is mistaken,' Carla said rather stiffly.

Meg thought it best to change the subject before they got into troubled waters and she asked Carla where she lived in Nether Rawcliffe. The mood between them relaxed a little before Meg took Carla downstairs to say goodbye to Mrs Peacock.

When the visitor had gone, Mrs Peacock was agog with interest to hear why Carla had come but Meg wasn't sure how much to say. In the end, she said very little but for the rest of the day she was thoughtful about the things Carla had said and implied.

* * *

Meg had started her evenings at the Youth Club and found that she loved it. Andrew usually looked in and often had a game of table tennis. There was no time for any personal conversation or contact, with a crowd of fifteen to twenty youngsters about them, but she felt by the look in his eyes that he was glad she was there and pleased with what she was doing to help.

But the chance of getting to know him a little better soon occurred and it happened on a Friday afternoon when she was expecting Geoffrey to call. As usual after lunch, she made her way up to the moor. She didn't vary her walk a lot and it had become an enjoyable routine to her. She was only put out when Geoffrey appeared. She thought she was going to have his company that day when she saw a figure climbing up the steeper part of the path towards the stones.

Then, on looking closer, she realised that it was not Geoffrey, but Andrew. She could just see the small band of his dog collar underneath his blue shirt. She felt both relief that it wasn't Geoffrey and pleasure that it was Andrew.

'You've chosen a lovely spot for yourself here,' he said as he sat down beside her. 'You can see right up the dale. Mrs Peacock said that I would find you here.'

'You don't usually visit her in the afternoon,' Meg remarked shyly.

'No, but I haven't come to see her. I've come to see you.'

It was said in such a personal and special way that it made Meg feel warm and flustered at the same time.

'There's never enough time after morning service or at the club to speak to you and I had an hour to spare so I thought I would come and hope to find you in. There is something I want to ask you.'

'You've got me curious.' She laughed.

'Well, I want to invite you and Jill to lunch after the service on Sunday. I've had an idea for the Youth Club and I want to talk it over with you both.'

If Meg felt a little sinking of disappointment, she didn't show it.

'I'd love to come,' she said. 'It happens to be my Sunday off and I don't always know what to do with myself.'

'Good,' he said. 'We'll meet up after the service and go back to the vicarage.'

He stopped speaking and looked around him.

'I could sit here all day talking to you but I must be on my way back. Are you coming, too?'

He had risen to his feet and put out a hand to her. She puts hers into it and felt his fingers close around hers. The touch was electric and once again she experienced that same magnetic feeling towards him. It was almost excitement that she felt but she tried to speak calmly.

'Yes, it's time for me to go back. My hour is up. Sometimes I wonder if I shall still come up here in the depths of winter. I imagine we get quite a lot of snow.'

They started walking down the hill.

'Yes. We're usually cut off at least once during the winter,' Andrew replied. 'Sometimes I haven't been able to get through to the other villages on a Sunday.'

When they reached the house, Meg could hear voices from the hall. Geoffrey had arrived. She had forgotten for the moment that it was his afternoon for coming to see Mrs Peacock.

The two men knew each other and shook hands. Geoffrey looked at Meg curiously. She seemed to have a glow about her and his manner was rather stiff and formal as he greeted Andrew.

'You've been up on the moor,' he said.

Meg was surprised at his tone and thought she had better be honest.

'Yes. Andrew had something to ask me and Mrs Peacock sent him out to look for me.' Then she turned to Andrew. 'Goodbye, Andrew, I'll see you on Sunday.'

Andrew left and Geoffrey still seemed surly.

'What are you meeting him for?' he asked.

Meg felt annoyed.

'It's nothing whatever to do with you what I do in my spare time,' she replied. 'But you might as well know that Jill Burnett and I are having lunch with Andrew to discuss the Youth Club.'

'I don't know why you had to get involved in that!'

Meg fumed but she was saved from

answering as Mrs Peacock called from the living-room. Geoffrey said no more and went to see his aunt.

After he had gone, Meg thought about his seeming jealousy of Andrew. It's quite ridiculous, she said to herself. I don't know what he's thinking about. She dismissed it from her mind and found herself looking forward to Sunday lunchtime.

When she got to church, she couldn't see Jill anywhere and after the service, she waited until Andrew had finished chatting to people as they left the church before asking where Jill was.

'Meg, there you are,' he said at last. 'Sorry, I got tied up. I hope you won't mind being the only one at lunch-time. Jill had a phone call from her father this morning to say that her mother wasn't well so she's gone over to Leeds. I don't think it's anything serious but she thought she ought to go. Just a minute, I'll see that everything's all right and then I'll be with you.'

He soon joined her and, leaving her

car where it was parked, they started to walk to the vicarage, a gracious, stone house not unlike Melbeck House, to the rear of the church.

'Isn't the vicarage rather big for you?' she asked him.

'Yes, it is really. I don't use all the rooms. It was built for a family. Perhaps one day, you never know,' he said with a grin. 'I have someone to come in and clean for me but I do all my own cooking so you needn't worry about lunch. I've put a chicken casserole in the oven.'

Meg enjoyed the meal. It was relaxed and friendly and she congratulated Andrew on his cooking.

'What was it you wanted to see me and Jill about?' she asked over a coffee.

'Well, I explained briefly to her on the phone this morning and she sounded quite keen. I'm wondering if we couldn't hire a mini-bus and take the youngsters on a day trip during the summer. We don't usually open the club in August because a lot of them are on holiday but a day out at the end of the summer term would be nice, wouldn't it? What do you think and would you be prepared to come and help?'

'It's a smashing idea. Where are you thinking of taking them?'

'I thought of the coast but it's rather a long way, so I wondered about Flamingoland, near Pickering. They'd love that. Those hair-raising rides they have are always a great attraction. Have you ever been there?'

'I remember going once when I was younger. I believe it's grown into quite a place now. The kids would love it, I'm sure.'

'Good, so you agree in principle and so does Jill. It's just a question of asking at the next club meeting if they are keen and then hiring a mini-bus, with a driver.'

He stopped and she found he was looking at her with a question in his eyes.

'Meg, I have to go up to Wedder Head to take evensong this afternoon. I wanted to ask you if you'd like to come and then we'll have a walk afterwards. There's quite a view.'

Meg was silent. She longed to say yes, but she couldn't forget Jill. On the other hand, it was only to a church service. There couldn't be a lot of harm in that!

'You are taking a long time to answer,' Andrew said.

'I was thinking about Jill,' Meg said truthfully.

'Oh, Jill's been up there lots of times,' he replied. 'I thought it would be rather nice just the two of us.'

Meg found it hard to understand the light-hearted tone of his remark but she said she would go and then insisted on doing the washing-up while he prepared for the service.

Andrew had changed out of his vestments when they had come back from the morning service and he packed up a bag to take up to Wedder Head.

They followed the river as far as Upper Rawcliffe and then the road got narrower and was no more than a country lane as it rose steeply to Wedder Head.

The church was tiny, not more than a dozen people making up the congregation. Andrew knew everyone and greeted them as they came in.

Meg found herself enjoying the simple service. It was peaceful and meaningful at the same time and her liking and admiration for Andrew seemed to grow.

They locked up the church after everyone had gone. Andrew had changed back into his denims and casual shirt, and as he put his hold-all in the boot of the car, he looked up at the sky.

'I hope it isn't going to rain,' he said. 'Are you fit for a walk up to Logan's Seat?'

He was pointing to the high ground behind the church.

'That's the name of that group of rocks that overlooks the village and gives such a splendid view of the dale.'

'I'd love to go. Hopefully the rain will hold off until we get back.'

They soon left the church and village behind them as they climbed up the steep path. Andrew didn't speak to her except once when he called to her not to look back yet.

It took them half an hour to reach the top and Meg flopped on the stones laughing and out of breath. Andrew laughed, too.

'I warned you it was steep. You can look back now.'

'Oh,' Meg said. 'Oh, it's beautiful.'

It was all she could say. They were high above Wedder Head and before them stretched the whole of Wedderdale.

'It's very clear today,' Andrew said. 'That's a sign of rain.'

'Pessimist.'

He grinned at her and Meg realised that she was enjoying this more than she would have thought possible. He began to point things out to her.

'If you follow the line of the river you can just see the roofs of Nether Rawcliffe.' He took her hand. 'Now look above those trees where the moor opens out. Do you see a building? That's High Aiskew, then look at those trees above. That's where Melbeck House is but you can't quite see it.'

On all sides the moorland dipped steeply towards the dale and in the centre was the thin silver line of the river.

'I never thought to see it all like this. Do you feel it's all yours, Andrew?' she said looking up at him.

'Well, that's one way of putting it. I suppose it is my responsibility and I go round and visit most of the farms. Even if they're not churchgoers, people still like to think they've got a vicar, someone to turn to if they are in trouble.'

'Oh, Andrew, you love it, don't you? Have you always been in a country parish?'

'No, after I was ordained, I was curate at a big city church in Bradford and when I knew my first parish was going to be Wedderdale, I had cold feet. I wondered how on earth I would cope with four churches and miles between each one.'

'But you love it,' she said again.

'Yes, I really do. It's hard work but I'm young and I don't mind that.'

'I do admire you, Andrew.'

Meg let the words slip out, straight from her heart.

'It couldn't be more than admiration, could it, Meg?' Andrew asked, looking fondly down at her.

'What do you mean?'

'I would like your friendship very much, Meg, but I feel your heart is elsewhere.'

'But, Andrew . . . ' she started to say, wondering what he meant and then she remembered Jill. He was asking for friendship, not love.

'We won't get ourselves involved. Let's just enjoy the view and then I'll race you back to the church,' he said cheerfully.

'I'm not racing anywhere,' she replied. 'Not down that steep path. And there's an enormous black cloud behind that hill!'

They hurried off down the hill and hadn't gone more than a few yards when they felt the first drops of heavy rain. Then the heavens opened while they were still on the open moor, with not a tree or a building in sight.

They were drenched in seconds and ran laughing, hand-in-hand, until they reached the car. Inside, with rain still thundering on the roof, they looked at each other and burst out laughing. Their clothes were clinging to them and their hair was streaming with water and plastered to their heads.

Andrew put out his arms towards her and Meg found herself falling into them. The contact was disastrous. She felt the warmth of his wet body close to hers, and as she raised her head to him, the kiss was inevitable. It was long and lingering, fierce yet gentle at the same time and Meg wanted it to go on for ever. They drew apart at last but were unable to stop gazing into each other's eyes.

'Meg,' Andrew whispered, 'I didn't mean for that to happen.'

'It's all right,' she said in a soft voice, thinking of Jill.

He pulled her against him and smoothed her wet head which she had rested against him.

'We'd better go home, Meg, and get dried off. You'll have to borrow some of my clothes.'

The commonsense remark brought them down to earth and Meg, knowing she had never felt such emotion before, was more than thankful for his sensible words. They drove quickly in silence back to the vicarage where no rain had fallen and the sun was just filtering through. Meg had a shower then dressed in an old pair of jeans of Andrew's and a cotton shirt. She rubbed her hair and combed it until it hung damp and shining about her shoulders. Then she found her way downstairs, where Andrew, also changed, was in the kitchen making tea.

He turned and smiled when he saw her.

'You look beautiful, Meg. I always knew you were attractive but in that blue shirt you look beautiful.'

'Andrew, you're teasing me.'

Meg had never felt more thankful that she was able to speak without giving away her feelings. The memory of the kiss was still burning within her and she longed to be on her own to savour the precious moment. Yet, at the same time, she wanted to be with Andrew, to talk to him, to get to know him better. Gladly she took the cup of tea from him and saw that he seemed to be determined to forget the episode at Wedder Head.

'We'll put your dress out on the line for half an hour,' he said. 'It should dry while we drink our tea. I don't want you going back to Melbeck House wearing my clothes.'

'Andrew, have you no fault? You always seem to say the right thing in the nicest possible way.'

He couldn't help laughing.

'Do you want me to list my faults for you? I am forgetful for a start. I remember to be at places on time then I find I've forgotten to take something that was vitally important. I think I need a wife to remind me. And I'm dreadfully untidy. You should have seen the tidying up I had to do before you came today!'

'Nothing worse than that?' she said, teasing him now.

But he was suddenly serious.

'I think my worst fault is that I'm sometimes intolerant. That sounds awful coming from a minister, doesn't it? But you know what I mean. If someone has behaved very badly, I'm quick to condemn them without really considering their point of view. I really have to fight it, Meg.'

'I think I'm quite relieved to know that you are not a saint,' she said with a smile, admiring his honesty.

'Will knowing all this make it easier for you to like me, Meg?'

'I do like you, Andrew. I like you very much.'

They were silent but it was an easy silence before the conversation turned more easily to plans for the Youth Club and the forthcoming trip.

Meg finally said goodbye and got back to Melbeck House soon after six. She told Mrs Peacock all about her day then went upstairs to be on her own. She had never felt so happy, yet had never felt so troubled in her conscience. She was walking on cloud nine and she knew that she had fallen in love with Andrew.

I really know I love him, she said to herself, and I know it's hopeless because of him and Jill. I must never show my feelings. I wouldn't come between them for the world but it won't be easy. Just for today, I'll allow myself to say it. I love Andrew.

She went to bed later that night with the sweet remembrance not only of his kiss but of the happy time they had spent together that day . . .

4

Meg's bubble of happiness burst exactly twenty-four hours later with a visit from Geoffrey. He came in the evening which was unusual and he seemed to be in an odd mood.

Mrs Peacock had gone to bed and Meg was sitting in the living-room where it was cooler than in her bedroom. It had been a hot, sunny day after the rain of the previous day.

'All on your own, Meg?' Geoffrey said as he entered the room.

'Yes, your aunt went up about half an hour ago. Did you want to see her?'

'No, I came to see you.'

She looked up quickly.

'Come out in the garden with me,' he went on. 'It will be cooler out there.'

His tone was light and friendly

but she could sense an undertone of seriousness. Nothing was said until they reached the seat under the tree where Meg sat down, rather curious. Geoffrey took hold of one of her hands and kept it clasped closely between both of his. She didn't wish for the contact but he started to speak before she had time to pull away.

'Meg, you don't need me to tell you that I've come to like you very much, do you? And I think we get on very well. No, don't say anything, just listen to what I have to say. As each day goes past, I can feel myself falling in love with you and I want to ask you if you will marry me.'

Meg was stunned into silence, not being able to believe that she had heard the words correctly. Marry Geoffrey? She turned to look at him. He was as handsome and charismatic as ever but there was a slight line of worry on his forehead and his eyes, while striving to be happy and unconcerned, contained a hidden expression of determination, almost desperation.

'Did you hear me, Meg?'

'I'm not sure,' was all she could say.

'I want you to marry me, Meg, marry me and come and live at High Aiskew. We could be so happy together, look forward to having a family and settling down.'

Was this really Geoffrey speaking, Meg thought. There must be something behind it all.

'What about Carla?' Meg asked, puzzled.

'Carla? What on earth has Carla got to do with it?'

'Carla came to see me a few days ago. She came to warn me off. She said she was going to marry you.'

Geoffrey's face flushed with anger.

'She couldn't have got it more wrong. I've known Carla a long time but there's never been a question of marriage. I would never marry Carla. I like her as a friend but I don't love her, and she can't have children.'

'And that's important to you, having children?'

Meg was beginning to get a clue to his unbelievable proposal of marriage.

'Of course it's important to me. We need an heir for High Aiskew . . . '

'And once you've got an heir, you'll be able to get all the money you want from Mrs Peacock?' Meg was beginning to get Geoffrey's measure. 'So that's why you are asking me to marry you.'

'Meg, for goodness' sake, I'm not as mercenary as that. You're a sweet girl, Meg. I would come to love you and you would love me. We could be very happy.'

'And what in the world makes you think that I could love you?'

Meg could see that she was winding Geoffrey up but she didn't care.

'Meg, look at me! Most girls fall for me without any prompting. And, eventually, I shall have Aunt Ethel's money. It would be a good marriage for anyone.'

'And you think that's all marriage requires? Good looks and plenty of money!'

'Well, yes, and you've got to get along. Well, we do get along, Meg.'

But Meg had worked out what Geoffrey Peacock was all about. He was obviously in financial trouble. He knew that if his aunt was happy about a marriage between him and Meg, then she would advance him some of the fortune. Carla was out of the picture and any moment now, Geoffrey would be urging Meg to marry him soon. She was right.

Geoffrey softened his tone and put an arm around her shoulders, stroking her arm.

'Meg, I'll say I love you if you want me to. I've never been so near to loving anyone in the whole of my life. Please say you'll marry me. We could be married in a month and have a lovely summer honeymoon somewhere. Meg, look at me and say yes.'

Meg did look at him. She shook his

hand away and faced him squarely.

'Geoffrey Peacock, you are the most self-opinionated and unprincipled man it has ever been my misfortune to meet. You want to marry me to get yourself out of financial difficulties. Do you think I don't know you? Well, the answer is no. I wouldn't marry you if you were the last man on earth.'

His face was scarlet with anger.

'You bitch! I know what it is! You've fallen for that vicar. I saw your face, all starry-eyed, the other day. And a lot of good that will do you. He's been tied up for the last year with that girl who runs the Youth Club for him. You'll never get anywhere with him and what's a vicar's stipend when I can offer you a fortune?'

Meg jumped up.

'Don't you ever think of anything except money? Is there no decency in you? I don't want to see you ever again. I shall make sure that I'm out of the way when you come on a Friday and don't try to pester me with your attentions, either.'

He was standing facing her, anger in his eyes.

'You are nothing but a harpy! I'll have my own back on you, just wait and see. There's no-one spurns Geoffrey Peacock and doesn't pay the price. Just remember those words, my girl.'

He stalked off down the garden leaving Meg sinking back on to the seat, trembling. She didn't know she had it in her to be so rude. She was ashamed but he had made her so angry. She tried to think of Andrew, but the selfish, greedy face of Geoffrey got in the way and she sat there, tears streaming down her face, until the evening got cold and she went indoors shivering.

Meg couldn't get Geoffrey out of her mind and the next day she thought she must talk to someone or burst. It was her Saturday off, so she gave Jill a ring and was pleased to find that her friend wasn't doing anything more urgent than a spot of gardening.

Meg took the car down into the village and Jill suggested that they drove round to neighbouring Garthdale and walk up on to the moor.

They went in Meg's car and parked in a quiet lane. The path from the lane to the moor was very steep. They were soon walking through heather. Both girls were silent, saving their breath for their exertions but both enjoying the exercise and the fresh air. When they got to the top, they threw themselves on to the heather, triumphant at having reached the top and delighting in the view.

'You can see Hexton,' Jill said, pointing to the roofs of a small town in the distance.

Meg looked all around her, seeing the farms on the other side of the dale and wondering if you could see Wedderdale.

'That's Logan's Seat,' Jill said, 'the hill above Wedder Head. You can just see the group of stones at the top. Have you been up there?'

Meg nodded and felt guilty.

'Andrew took me up there that Sunday when you went to see your mother. He was taking the evening service at Wedder Head.'

Jill looked at her.

'Do you like Andrew, Meg?' she asked suddenly.

'Yes, I think he is a very nice person,' Meg answered cautiously.

'I think he's the nicest person I've ever met,' Jill said with enthusiasm. 'I thought he was falling for you.'

Meg looked at her keenly. Jill hadn't sounded in the least concerned or jealous. What did it mean? She decided it best to avoid the subject.

'It's not Andrew I'm having trouble with,' she said. 'It's Geoffrey Peacock.'

Jill look astonished.

'Geoffrey Peacock? But I thought you liked him! He's so attractive and all the village is matchmaking between the pair of you. Saying it's the best thing that's ever happened.'

Meg laughed aloud.

'The village can say what it likes, but they are quite wrong. I wanted to talk to you about it, Jill. Do you mind?'

'No, of course not. Whatever's happened?'

'I've been in such a state. Geoffrey came to the house and asked me to marry him. I knew straight away that it was just so that he could get his hands on the money from Mrs Peacock. It's all he thinks about. We had a dreadful quarrel. He seemed to think we would get to love one another. Would you marry without love, Jill?' Meg asked.

'Definitely not, never. I've never told anyone, but I love someone very much but he sees me just as a friend. If I can't marry him then I shall remain a spinster school teacher all my life.'

She must mean Andrew, Meg thought. He is certainly very friendly towards her but I thought there was more in it than that. That makes two of us, both in love with Andrew. But she mustn't say what she was thinking.

'You should have patience, Jill,' she

said. 'He must surely get to love you one day.'

Jill sighed.

'Sometimes it seems hopeless but I'm not eating my heart out over a man who doesn't love me. I've got a good job, I've got the Youth Club and now I've got you for a friend so I'm not doing so badly.'

She looked at Meg.

'So you're not going to marry Geoffrey?'

'Not if he was the last man on earth and I told him so. He wasn't very pleased. He said he would get his own back on me but I don't know what he meant by that.'

'Sounds rather sinister.'

'It's only because I've stopped him getting hold of the money.'

'I always thought he was going to marry Carla Handley. They've been close for years,' Jill remarked.

'I think he considers that she's too old for him. All he can think about is getting an heir to the Peacock fortune.

Don't be surprised if he tries to get round you next!'

Jill was amused.

'No, we've hardly met and we didn't like each other. I thought he was conceited and he thought I was prissy.'

Meg couldn't stop herself laughing.

'Oh, you are good for me. I'm so glad we came here. It's been really nice. And we've not talked about the Youth Club. What do you think about Andrew's idea for a summer trip?'

'It's great,' Jill replied. 'We'll have to start organising soon. It's getting near the end of term and we've got to hire the mini-bus. You'll be able to come, won't you?'

'I hope so. It depends if it's my Saturday off or not though I expect Mrs Coates would always change with me. I wouldn't want to miss it.'

They talked on about the school and the club before they walked slowly back to the car. Meg felt much happier to have talked about her dilemma but still had the conviction that Jill and

Andrew would make a match of it very soon. She tried hard to bury her own feelings.

The next few days were quiet, with no more sign of Geoffrey, but following a usual Friday visit to Mrs Peacock by him Mrs Peacock felt ill. Meg had stayed out of the way until Geoffrey had gone, but that evening, after their meal, when Meg went into the living-room to see if Mrs Peacock was ready to go upstairs, she found the old lady almost doubled up in her wheel-chair, her hand on her stomach.

'What is it, Mrs Peacock?' Meg asked, running to her side.

'I don't know, Meg. I've got awful pains in my stomach and I feel very sick. It must be something I've eaten but I can't imagine what we've had that would cause an upset.'

'Would you like me to call the doctor?'

'Oh, dear, no. I'll take some warm milk and go to bed. I'm sure I'll feel better in the morning.'

But Mrs Peacock had an uncomfortable night although she insisted she felt well enough to get up and get dressed and go downstairs the following morning. She looked pale and drawn and Meg felt worried.

Without saying anything, she rang Dr Sinclair at his Hexton surgery. He listened carefully and promised he would come up to Melbeck House later in the day. It didn't sound as though it was anything urgent.

Meg went and told Mrs Peacock what she had done and was relieved that her patient made no objections. When he arrived that afternoon, Mrs Peacock was feeling much better and was apologetic.

'I feel guilty getting you out, Doctor Sinclair,' she said. 'I'm sure it was just something I'd eaten.'

He examined her carefully and was not alarmed.

'I think it's more likely to be the side effects of all those drugs you are on for your arthritis. Anti-inflammatory drugs are notorious for causing stomach problems though I did think that we'd managed to find one that suited you. I am not going to alter your drugs for you are doing well on them but I will leave you with a mixture to take if you get any more pain. If it gets worse, you are to make sure to call me.'

Mrs Peacock improved quickly after that but seemed to get an attack about once a week. The medicine seemed to help and she soon recovered each time. However, Meg was puzzled by the attacks. They seemed to follow a regular pattern and she and Mrs Coates racked their brains to try and think of which foods could possible have upset the old lady.

Several weeks went by. The Youth Club trip to Flamingoland came and went and was a great success. When the Youth Club closed for the summer holidays, a weekly ramble continued when any of the youngsters could join Jill and Andrew on Andrew's day off. Sometimes, Meg managed to join them for part of the walk and Andrew always seemed pleased to see her.

In August, Meg decided to take a week off. She had arranged to visit her sister who lived with her family in Whitby and an agency nurse came to look after Mrs Peacock while she was away. But her patient was very glad to see her back again after the holiday.

Meg came back to find Mrs Peacock recovering from one of her attacks, then the following Friday, she had another one. With a blinding flash, Meg suddenly realised that something had been staring her in the face and only her absence had made her aware of the significance of it. Mrs Peacock's attacks always occurred within an hour or two of Geoffrey's Friday visit!

She was walking up on the moor when she thought of it and stared across the dale, wondering whatever could be the significance of her discovery. Was Geoffrey deliberately upsetting his aunt to make her ill, or was it just coincidence? What could she do about it? Should she ask Mrs Peacock?

She put all these questions to herself and thought about it for a long time, in the end deciding to watch and listen very carefully when Geoffrey paid his regular visits.

On the very next Friday, she heard Mrs Coates let Geoffrey in and then the rattle of tea cups as the tea tray was carried through. Once Mrs Coates was safely back in the kitchen, Meg stationed herself quietly outside the living-room door and listened carefully.

'Sugar, Aunt Ethel?'

'Yes, please, dear.'

'And a piece of fruit cake. Mrs Manthorpe sent it up for you.'

'I'm not sure that I'm meant to have fruit cake but I'll have just a small piece. Now, what's your news this week, Geoffrey?'

Then followed the usual report about the farm and gossip about the village. It all sounded friendly and innocent and Meg almost tiptoed away, disappointed that her suspicions hadn't been right.

Then Geoffrey's next words caught her ear and she stood rooted to the spot.

'What is it, Aunt Ethel, that pain again?'

'Yes, I feel most uncomfortable.'

'Let me pour you some of your medicine. That should help.'

'Thank you, Geoffrey, then perhaps you'd better go, and we'll get Mrs Coates to go and look for Meg.'

Meg quickly disappeared up to her room, puzzled. Geoffrey was only giving Mrs Peacock some of her medicine — what was wrong with that? He had sounded quite kind and caring and she knew he could be like that if he wanted to. Nothing seemed to make sense and when Mrs Peacock had another attack later on that evening, Meg was at a loss to understand it. I'll see what happens next Friday, she said to herself.

But the following Friday, things went wrong from the start. Geoffrey arrived an hour earlier than usual, he was on edge and impatient, asking to see Meg immediately. She was reading a book in the garden when he came out of the back door and called her name.

'Meg, are you there?'

She looked up and saw that he was upset about something, the usual smooth good looks ruffled.

'Is Mrs Peacock all right? she asked, jumping up.

'I haven't seen her yet. I want to speak to you. Will you walk down the garden with me?'

She was reluctant but didn't want to refuse and make a scene.

By the time he started to talk to her, he seemed to have calmed down a little and she walked quietly by his side until they got to the gate at the bottom of the garden. He stopped her there with a strong hand on her arm.

'Meg, I know you have been avoiding me and, of course, I know why. But I want you to know that I've missed you, Meg. I've missed you more than I would have believed possible. It made me realise that I do love you and although I know you said some very harsh things the last time I asked, I want to ask you again. I love you, Meg. Would you marry me?'

She stared at him. The words had been soft and persuasive and had also seemed genuine, but somehow Meg could sense a tension in him and she had the feeling that if she refused him again then that tension would snap. Something about the situation made her feel afraid.

He must have misinterpreted her silence for suddenly he pulled her towards him, kissing her gently on the lips. It was a soft kiss, almost brotherly.

'You are going to say yes, Meg, please. Tell me you are going to say yes. You know that we could be happy together.'

'Geoffrey,' she said, trying to speak quietly, 'I do not love you and I am not going to marry you. In fact, you might as well know that I am in love with somebody else and if I can't marry him, I shall never marry anybody.'

Meg didn't like saying this but she hoped that it would convince him, but his patience and his softness broke.

'It's that Andrew Sheratt! You see him every week at the Youth Club, don't you? He'll never marry you. The whole village knows he is going to marry Jill Burnett, so why can't you marry me? Aunt Ethel will let me have the money if you marry me. She told me so. You've got to marry me, Meg, it's the only answer.'

She could hear the desperation in his voice and guessed that once again he had got himself into deep water.

'More gambling debts, Geoffrey?' she asked.

But Geoffrey wasn't quiet any longer. His voice was raised and he shouted at her.

'Yes, blast you, I am in debt. My only chance of getting out of debt is to marry you, Meg, unless Aunt Ethel dies sooner than we thought.'

'Mrs Peacock is not going to die.'

He took her by the arms again and

his fingers hurt her.

'Meg, I've got an idea. Would you pretend you are going to marry me? Let's go and tell her we are engaged. That would do the trick. She'd be so pleased she would write me a cheque straight away.'

Meg met his blazing eyes and thought she saw evil there. She braced herself to be strong.

'That's wicked, Geoffrey, and you know it. I wouldn't have any part in such a plan. You've brought this all on yourself. You could have stopped gambling at any time but you chose to think that your aunt would just advance you the money that will eventually come to you. Well, you were wrong.

'That money was hard-earned by the Peacocks over a long time and Mrs Peacock won't let it go to a wastrel like you. As for me, I'm not going to marry you and I'm not going to pretend to marry you. You can put it right out of your mind this minute. I'm going indoors and you can sort it out with your aunt but don't you dare upset her.'

'You'll regret this, my girl, you see if you don't. I'll get even with you yet. I'll cause you so much shame and trouble that even that vicar won't want to know you. You just wait and see.'

And she watched him stride off towards the house and disappear. She found she was trembling, but she couldn't see how he could possibly harm her if she kept out of his way. She tried to pull herself together, and walked slowly back to the house.

5

When Meg reached the house, she could hear raised voices coming from the living-room and guessed that, once again, Mrs Peacock and Geoffrey were quarrelling. Unashamedly she listened at the door.

'But, Aunt Ethel,' Meg heard Geoffrey saying, 'I'm desperate for the money and it would come to me one day in any case. It wouldn't do you any harm to advance me a few thousand.'

'I can guess it's more than a few thousand you need, Geoffrey, but you are not getting it. The money comes to you because you're the only surviving Peacock but I'll have you know that I can change my will at any time. In fact, I've had it changed recently.'

'What do you mean?' he asked nastily.

'I have decided to leave ten thousand

to Meg. It's not a lot but it will buy her a new car to replace that old banger of hers.'

Outside the door, Meg felt uncomfortable, overhearing something she wasn't supposed to know. She almost moved away but stood rooted to the spot, worried that Mrs Peacock was going to upset herself. She dared not go in.

'Meg, Meg, Meg! The blasted girl! If she'd only marry me, everything would work out fine. You'd like that, wouldn't you?' Geoffrey was saying.

'Yes, I must admit I would, though I must say that Meg deserves someone better than you.'

Meg could imagine Geoffrey's fury but Mrs Peacock went on.

'If you'd come in here to tell me that you and Meg were engaged it would have been a different matter. I think she would be a good influence on you and bring some stability to High Aiskew. Have you asked her?'

'Yes. I've asked her more than once. All she'll say is that she's in love with someone else. It must be that vicar of yours, I think.'

'Oh, I hope not, though they do get on very well, but I am sure he is going to marry the girl who is the infant teacher at the school.'

'That's what I told her but it doesn't make her change her mind. I'll ask you once more, Aunt Ethel. Could you see your way to letting me have about fifty thousand? You wouldn't even miss it.'

'I will not advance it to you, Geoffrey, and those are my last words on the subject. You can pour me out a cup of tea.'

Meg crept away. Mrs Peacock was well able to deal with her nephew and she felt guilty that she had listened for so long. Half an hour after Geoffrey had gone, Mrs Coates came running upstairs for Meg.

'Miss Meg, come quickly, it's the mistress! She's right queer . . . '

Meg ran downstairs and found Mrs Peacock doubled up in pain and in a cold sweat, asking for water.

'I must have a drink, Meg.'

'I'll give you some of your medicine, Mrs Peacock.'

'No, Geoffrey has already given me some. Just some water, please I must have some water.'

Mrs Coates hurried away while Meg phoned the surgery. Dr Sinclair had one more patient to see then would come straight away. Meg didn't know what to do for her poor patient while they waited for the doctor. She continually demanded drinks and was crying with the pain. Meg wondered if the doctor had been wrong and that the trouble had been an ulcer which had now burst.

Dr Sinclair was with them in little over half an hour and when he saw Mrs Peacock's condition, he looked grim. He questioned her about her medicine and asked to see it, tasting a little on his tongue. He examined her carefully and wiped her damp forehead, then he turned to Meg.

'Ring for an ambulance quickly. I

want her in hospital in Leeds. You can go with her.'

Meg rushed to do as she was bidden. The ambulance had to come from Hexton and then it would take an hour to get to Leeds. When she put the receiver down, she saw that Dr Sinclair had come out of the room to speak to her.

'What is it, Doctor Sinclair? Is it a burst ulcer? That was the only thing I could think of.'

'No, it's not an ulcer. It's my belief that Mrs Peacock has been poisoned. Her condition has all the signs of arsenic poisoning and I'm now wondering if it has been going on for some time and I didn't suspect it. You are to take her medicine with you for analysis. Don't look so worried, Meg. We might get her there in time. I'll wait until the ambulance arrives. There's nothing we can do but give her plenty of drinks.'

Meg felt as though she had been hit by something really hard. She could hardly take in what he was saying. Poison? Thoughts and impressions rushed through her mind leaving her quite bewildered. Friday afternoons? Geoffrey? Had he been trying to poison his aunt, giving her small doses of the poison so that the final and fatal dose would arouse no suspicion? Had he been planning it to get at her money?

Today had been the last straw for him. He must have been relying on Meg to help him out of his troubles so that he wouldn't have to take the final desperate measure. And that afternoon had brought her refusal to marry him or to pretend to an engagement and Mrs Peacock's refusal to let him have any money.

These dreadful thoughts whirled about in Meg's mind and she didn't know if she should tell Dr Sinclair of her suspicions.

But he had gone back into the room and five minutes later, the ambulance arrived. Dr Sinclair saw her off and told her that he would get in touch with Geoffrey Peacock.

Meg thought that Mrs Peacock was going to die before they reached the hospital. She was holding her hand but the old lady was only semiconscious. The paramedic kept giving her sips of water and once they were on the main road to Leeds, Meg was aware of their much increased speed.

The hospital was expecting them and had a room ready. The next couple of hours were lost to Meg but she knew that Mrs Peacock had had her stomach pumped out and was now lying unconscious, connected to a drip. Meg was given a bed in a nearby room but she couldn't sleep and kept creeping back to see if Mrs Peacock was still alive.

'She's a little better,' the night nurse whispered. 'She seems to be sleeping more naturally now.'

So Meg snatched a few hours sleep, haunted with the nightmares of what had happened. She was very restless and every time she stirred, she would think of Geoffrey. She felt now that she had not imagined the evil look in Geoffrey's eyes that afternoon and that he had been planning this for some time, if he was not able to get hold of the money by any other means.

She got up early, had a quick wash, then she tiptoed to Mrs Peacock's room, dreading what she might find. But the old lady was still sleeping peacefully and the nurse said that her pulse and heart were steady. She made Meg go along to the nurses' kitchen to make herself some tea or coffee and Meg was glad of the hot, strong drink.

Later she managed to eat some toast at breakfast time and began to feel stronger and more hopeful. She sat in the corner of the small ward and waited for a movement from the bed. A little while later, a doctor came in, looked at the patient and then called Meg outside.

'I understand you are Mrs Peacock's nurse,' he said. 'She suffers badly from arthritis,' I believe.

'Yes,' Meg nodded.

'I have to tell you that we have just had the laboratory report and quite a quantity of arsenic has been found in the medicine you brought in. There were also traces of arsenic found in the stomach. You realise that this is a serious matter?'

Meg felt as though things were swimming round her and the doctor directed her to a seat.

'It's a matter for the police. Has Mrs Peacock any close relatives? They should be informed, as she is not out of danger yet.'

Meg told him about Geoffrey but did not mention her suspicions or anything about Geoffrey's circumstances. She felt herself quite unable to come to terms with the fact that Mrs Peacock had been deliberately poisoned.

The doctor was still speaking.

'She was given a dose that was obviously meant to kill her but in spite of her arthritic condition, she has a very strong constitution and is fighting back very well. I see no reason why should not make a complete recovery. You have been close to her all these months, Nurse Bowering, and the police will wish to speak to you. Please don't go from the ward.'

He stopped and looked at her, a pretty, sensible-looking girl, surely not capable of trying to murder her elderly patient. There was some mystery here but it was not for him to delve into. He tried to put Meg more at ease.

'Go and have some coffee then I would be glad if you would sit with the nurse who is attending Mrs Peacock. She will need to see a familiar face when she wakes up but I don't want you to mention anything about the poison. She will need to know later on but for the time being let her think it is something we are still investigating. She will simply think that the drugs she has been on have caused her attack and that is the best thing for the moment. I have given instructions that I am to be called as soon as Mrs Peacock wakes up. OK?'

'Yes, thank you, doctor.'

Meg only managed to murmur the words but after he had gone, she took his advice and got some coffee and took it to her little room. Suddenly she heard a voice.

'I think you will find her in here,' it said and she looked up to see Andrew standing in the doorway.

She put down her coffee mug and stood up, unable to believe that it could possibly be him here in the hospital just at the very moment when she really needed him.

'Andrew.'

She threw herself at him and found herself caught in a tight grip, his mouth against her hair, whispering her name.

'Meg, are you all right?'

She came to her senses and broke away from him, embarrassed, but he had put an arm round her shoulders and led her to the bed where he sat down by her side. She looked into his kindly, sympathetic eyes and felt tears slide down her cheeks. He took a handkerchief from his pocket and wiped them away.

'Tell me, Meg. Tell me all about it.'

'Andrew, how did you get here? How did you know?'

'Dr Sinclair phoned me last night so I came as soon as I could this morning. How is Mrs Peacock?'

'The doctor has just told me that she has fought back very well and they expect her to recover. I am to go and sit with her in a minute but I must talk to you first. I don't seem to be able to think straight. What did Dr Sinclair tell you?'

'He said that she was ill with arsenic poisoning which he thought had been deliberately administered. It's very serious, Meg.'

'I know, I know and I have to talk to the police soon and I don't know what to say.'

Meg was very distressed and Andrew

held her hands tightly between his own.

'Do you know anything about it then?' he asked.

'I don't know. I have my suspicions but they are so dreadful that I cannot even voice them.'

She buried her head against his shoulder and again the tears came.

'Meg, I've got to say this in case you haven't even thought of it. You know that you will be a suspect, don't you?'

She looked up quickly at that.

'Me? But I didn't do it. How could I have done it? You know I wouldn't have done such a thing, don't you, Andrew?'

'I know you wouldn't have done it but the police don't know you as I do. You are a suspect to them as you have been the nearest person to Mrs Peacock for many months.'

He spoke calmly and quietly and she tried to take his words in.

'Have you any idea who could have done it, Meg?'

She nodded but did not speak.

'Do you want to tell me?' he asked.

'It is so dreadful I don't think I can speak about it,' she replied in a hushed voice.

'Then I will ask you and you can just nod. Does it have anything to do with Geoffrey Peacock?'

She sat quite still at his question but then nodded her head very slowly.

'Does he have a lot to gain from his aunt's death?'

Again the nod.

'And why do you suspect him?'

She turned and clung to him and again he held her. Words came at last and she spoke quickly though very quietly.

'It was because Mrs Peacock was always ill after his visits on a Friday afternoon. I couldn't understand it. Then he asked me to marry him so that she would advance him some money. She wanted me to marry him so that there would be a Peacock here.'

'And you said?'

'I said I wouldn't and he was angry. Yesterday he asked me again and I still said no then, after he had gone, Mrs Peacock became so ill and I didn't know what to think. When Dr Sinclair said that he thought it was poisoning, I couldn't but help suspect Geoffrey. But I can't be sure. What shall I say to the police, Andrew? Oh, please help me. And don't tell anyone what I've said, will you? I would only ever have told it to you, no-one else.'

'Don't forget you are talking to a minister, Meg. Your secret is safe with me. What you have told me is only a suspicion, though. You cannot be sure, and it would be wrong to accuse another person just because of a suspicion. So when the police come, answer their questions honestly. If they ask you about Geoffrey then you must tell them. Just be honest, Meg.'

'Thank you, Andrew, you have helped me a lot. I don't feel quite so afraid now. Shall we go and see if Mrs Peacock has woken up yet?'

They sat with the nurse at Mrs Peacock's bedside for quite some time before she stirred. When she opened her eyes, Meg gripped Andrew's hand. The old lady looked round her, obviously puzzled. She saw the nurse first, then her eyes lighted on Meg and Andrew and she gave a tiny smile.

'Meg. Andrew. Wherever am I? What time is it? And what are you both doing here?'

The nurse had rung for the doctor and he was there in minutes, talking quietly, reassuring, doing all that needed to be done.

'You are in hospital in Leeds, Mrs Peacock,' he told her. 'You were brought in with severe stomach pains. I understand that you have been having tummy trouble lately.'

They waited to see if she would understand.

'Oh, yes. Dr Sinclair thought that it was the side effects of the drugs I was on. Was he wrong?'

The doctor smiled, pleased at her

sensible approach.

'No, he was not wrong but we think that they may have caused an ulcer. We can treat you easily for that. There will be no need for an operation, just a couple of days rest and a change of medicine. Now I will let you talk to your friends for ten minutes, then you must rest again. The nurse will stay with you.'

He patted her hand and smiled at her and was gone. Mrs Peacock turned to Meg.

'You came in the ambulance with me. I remember now. But, Andrew, how did you get here?'

'I came to see my favourite parishioner as soon as I knew she was ill, Mrs Peacock. It is good to see you so bright.'

'Yes, I am feeling better. The pain has gone but I feel so weak. I think I will have another sleep now.'

She drifted off to sleep and Meg and Andrew sat back and smiled at each other with relief.

The next time she woke, she managed to sip some warm milk and some colour had come back into her cheeks.

'Andrew, I mustn't keep you here,' she said. 'Saturday is always a busy day for you with your services to prepare. It was very kind of you to come.'

'It's all right, Mrs Peacock. It's still quite early. I just wanted to stay until I knew you were on the mend.'

'Well, I am on the mend.' Mrs Peacock managed a smile and then looked at Meg. 'Hasn't Geoffrey come? Does he know?'

Meg's heart missed a beat but she managed to sound quite unconcerned.

'Dr Sinclair said he would let him know last night so I expect he will be along later today.'

'Hm,' the old lady grunted. 'Strange that Andrew could manage to get here first thing but not my nephew. But I don't suppose I shall ever understand Geoffrey.'

Andrew stood up then and took her hand.

'I'd better be on my way now. It's good to see you getting better. Meg will stay with you and when you are well enough to come home, if Geoffrey can't fetch you, I will come back for you. As long as it's not a Sunday morning!'

They all smiled. Mrs Peacock lay back against the pillows and closed her eyes. Meg went with Andrew to see him off. They stood together in the entrance hall of the hospital.

'I don't know what I should have done without you, Andrew,' Meg said.

'I'm glad I was able to come. Will you be able to manage when Geoffrey turns up?' he asked her.

'Yes, I think so. I shall let him see Mrs Peacock on his own.'

'Good girl. When I get home, I'll give Mrs Coates a ring to tell her the news. She'll be worrying, won't she?'

'I should have thought of that,' Meg said ruefully.

'You've got enough on your mind. You can ring me at any time. I'll probably be writing sermons for the rest of the day!'

'Oh, Andrew, I'll never be able to thank you enough.'

'You don't have to.'

He grinned, and pulled her towards him and kissed her on the cheek then lightly touched her lips with his own.

She watched him disappear in the direction of the car park. Andrew Sheratt, she said to herself, Jill is a very, very lucky person . . .

Geoffrey didn't turn up that morning but the police did.

Meg was sitting with Mrs Peacock, whose periods of wakefulness were getting longer and longer, when the doctor she had seen the previous evening tapped her on the shoulder. She got up and followed him out. He led her into an office where a tall man and a dark-haired girl were standing.

'Nurse Bowering, this is Detective Sergeant Boyes and Detective Constable Woodleigh. They have come to interview Mrs Peacock but I will not permit it.

I have told them that you will be able to tell them all they need to know. You can use the table, sergeant. I will leave you.'

Meg felt incredibly nervous but the young woman constable seemed to understand.

'Don't worry, Nurse Bowering, it's just some preliminary information we need to know about the patient and as the doctor said, she is not fit to be questioned yet. You will probably be able to tell us all we need to know.'

Meg nodded.

'She is Ethel Mary Peacock, aged seventy-nine, of Melbeck House, Nether Rawcliffe, near Hexton.'

'Yes.'

'Her husband is no longer living?'

'No.'

'And has she any children? If not, who is her closest relative?'

'She never had any children, and her closest relative is her nephew.'

'Mr Geoffrey Peacock of High Aiskew Farm?'

'Yes.'

'It is his farm?'

'No, it is Mrs Peacock's farm. It was her late husband's and his father's before that. Geoffrey runs it for her.'

'He is married?'

'No.'

'Did he see his aunt regularly? Were they on good terms?'

Dangerous ground here, Meg thought, but she stayed calm.

'He usually came to see her every Friday afternoon, to give her a report about the farm.'

'And their relationship?'

Careful, Meg said to herself.

'It was generally very good,' she replied.

'Why do you say generally?'

'I'd rather not say.'

'Very well. And now tell me something about yourself.'

And so the questions went on. They seemed endless. How long had she been at Melbeck House? Where had she been before? Did she get on well

116

with Mrs Peacock or was she a difficult patient?

Meg didn't find the questions difficult to answer and she was honest about all they asked her, not hiding anything from them, but all the time she was somehow waiting for them to trap her. However, the interview came to an end and she was told that they would keep in touch with her and would come and see Mrs Peacock at Melbeck House as soon as she was well enough to be interviewed.

By the time it had all finished, Meg felt exhausted and finding Mrs Peacock asleep on her return to the ward, she lay down on her own bed and slept till lunchtime. All that afternoon, she expected to see Geoffrey and Mrs Peacock kept asking for him. She had eaten a light lunch and had a sleep afterwards and was almost looking her old self.

Eventually, Meg could stand the suspense no longer and decided to phone the farm. Surely Geoffrey would be there and she could ask him if he was coming. Mrs Manthorpe answered the phone.

'Hello, Miss Meg, how's Mrs Peacock . . . that's good . . . no, he's not here. He packed up a case and went off in the car first thing this morning. He didn't say a lot, seemed worried which I could understand with his poor aunt being taken off to hospital like that. No, I thought he'd gone off to stay in Leeds to be near Mrs Peacock.'

When Meg finally put down the receiver, she was very puzzled. What on earth had happened to Geoffrey? He should have been here by now. While she was at the phone, she spoke to Mrs Coates and reassured her that all was well. She learned that the police had been to see Mrs Coates as well but had not asked anything out of the ordinary — just how long she'd been at Melbeck House and if she knew anything about relations between Mr Peacock and his aunt.

She told them that he visited once

a week and seemed on good terms, but she didn't say anything about the gambling. She didn't think it had anything to do with Mrs Peacock's illness and it was certainly no business of theirs. Finding out about the poison had come as a shock to her and she told Meg she'd suspected Mr Geoffrey, but she hadn't said so to the police. After asking when Mrs Peacock would be home, she hung up.

Meg put down the receiver very thoughtfully. So she was not the only one to think badly of Geoffrey and there was no doubt that he had had a very strong motive. But to try to kill his aunt — surely even Geoffrey wasn't evil enough to do that . . .

6

Geoffrey had still not turned up at the hospital and Meg spent the rest of the day awaiting his arrival nervously, wondering how she was going to confront him. She just could not understand where he was and why he hadn't come. The only bright spot in the whole day was that Mrs Peacock improved by the hour, and by evening, she was able to sit in a wheel-chair and watch television.

Sunday morning came and still there was no sign of Geoffrey. Mrs Peacock, however, was continuing to improve and Meg began to wonder if she would be allowed home that day. Just before lunch, Meg had a surprise visitor when the nurse came to tell her that a Miss Jill Burnett was in the day room. Feeling very pleased, Meg hurried along and found Jill with David Courtney, the headmaster of the village school.

'Meg!' Jill gave her a hug and they all sat down. 'Andrew says that he's sorry he can't come but he's got services in all the churches today. I found out that David was bringing his two girls into Leeds to go ice-skating and he said he would bring me to the hospital. The girls are in the car so we mustn't be long.'

She looked searchingly at Meg.

'How is Mrs Peacock? There are all sorts of rumours flying around the village. Someone even said that she was poisoned. We didn't know whether to believe it or not and I haven't had a chance to ask Andrew the truth of it.'

Meg looked dubious. It looked as though Mrs Coates or Mrs Manthorpe had said something. How else would anyone know?

'I'll have to be truthful,' she said to them. 'She was brought into the hospital suffering from arsenic poisoning. That's all I'm prepared to say and I'd rather you didn't repeat it. Mrs

Peacock doesn't know it was that. I'm glad to say that she's a lot better this morning.'

David spoke for the first time.

'Is there anything we can do to help?' he asked.

Meg shook her head.

'Just tell people that Mrs Peacock is a lot better and will soon be home. It was very kind of you to bring Jill, David. I'm really pleased to see you.'

They left then and Meg stood thinking what a nice person David was and what a tragedy it had been about his wife. It looked as though Mrs Peacock had been right when she had said that Jill helped him with the girls at the week-ends.

Meg spent the rest of the day sitting with Mrs Peacock but was unable to get Geoffrey out of her mind. Every time someone came in the door, she expected it to be him but there was no sign of him.

By tea-time, the doctor said that Mrs Peacock could go home as long as she had Dr Sinclair to visit her and that Meg was with her all the time. Meg phoned Geoffrey again but there was no reply at all from the farm, so she spoke to Andrew. With his Sunday services over, he said he would come over to Leeds straight away.

By nine o'clock, Mrs Peacock was safely back home. Both she and Mrs Coates cried when they saw each other again.

Meg went to the gate with Andrew.

'I don't know what's happened to Geoffrey,' she said to him.

'He didn't turn up?'

'No, not at all, and he's not at the farm. Mrs Peacock was upset that he hadn't been to see her so I kept phoning. Mrs Manthorpe said that he'd gone off on Saturday morning and he's not been seen since.'

'It sounds very suspicious to me,' Andrew said.

'I don't know what to make of it. I suppose we'll have the police here again.' Meg looked at Andrew. 'I shall have to tell them, Andrew.'

'Yes, I think you will. His disappearance is certainly very strange. Don't be afraid of ringing if you want me, Meg. I can be up here in ten minutes.'

'Thanks, Andrew. You're the only sane thing in my life at the moment.'

He squeezed her hand and gave a grin.

'I don't know that I like being described as a thing,' he said, 'but as long as I can be of help that's all that matters. You mean a lot to me, Meg.'

With these words, he was off, leaving Meg to wonder exactly what he meant, if he meant anything at all. It was the sort of nice thing that Andrew would say. She sighed and went indoors again.

Next morning, Meg was up early and even before she had taken Mrs Peacock some breakfast, she found Dr Sinclair on the doorstep.

'What brings you here?' she asked.

'Mrs Peacock's fine, she's had a good night and I'm going to take her a light breakfast. Are you worried about her diet?'

'No, it's not that. We've got to tell her about the arsenic, Meg, and I thought it would be better coming from me.'

Meg had expected that but she felt very worried. She thanked the doctor for coming and asked rather tentatively, 'Can I be with you when you tell her?'

'Yes, I think that would be wise. It's going to come as a great shock to her.'

They went upstairs and Dr Sinclair sat himself by Mrs Peacock's side, his hand on her pulse. Meg stood behind him, her eyes fixed on Mrs Peacock's face.

'Mrs Peacock.' Dr Sinclair spoke very quietly and calmly. 'I've come to tell you something that is going to come as rather a shock to you. We have known about it all along but you weren't strong enough to be told in the first place.'

The indomitable old lady glared at him.

'I'm going to die, is that what it is?'

In spite of the gravity of the situation, Dr Sinclair couldn't stop a chuckle escaping.

'No, you are not going to die, not for many years, I hope. But when you had those dreadful pains on Friday, and the doctor in the hospital told you that he thought it was an ulcer, he was not telling you the truth. You haven't got an ulcer. The pains were caused because you had been given arsenic. There were traces of arsenic found in your medicine. It didn't kill you but I think it was meant to.'

Mrs Peacock had gone deathly white and Dr Sinclair kept his finger on her wrist, turning to Meg at the same time.

'Get her a cup of tea, Meg, but not too hot.'

Meg did as she was told and when she got back she found Mrs Peacock talking to Dr Sinclair. The old lady seemed glad of the tea and turned to Meg.

'It's a shock, Meg, I don't mind telling you. Did you do it?'

Meg swallowed hard.

'No, I didn't Mrs Peacock.'

'I believe you. Have you any idea who did?'

'No, no. I'm not sure, I'm not sure at all.'

'Don't dither, girl. You think it was Geoffrey, and I think it was Geoffrey. He was after my money. I wouldn't give it to him so he thought that if I was out of the way, he'd soon get the lot. It's as plain as a pikestaff and I shall tell the police so. He's my nephew and he's a Peacock but he's a bad 'un, always has been. No, Doctor Sinclair, I'm not getting excited. I've survived, haven't I, but what will happen to Geoffrey? No wonder he didn't come to the hospital. He probably went out of the country when he found out I was all right. They'll never find him.'

Dr Sinclair stopped her at last.

'Mrs Peacock, you've taken the news very well but it's still a shock and I'm going to give you a light sedative. Then you can have your breakfast but you are not to get up until this afternoon. I'll come back this evening. Do you understand all that?'

She lay back on her pillows suddenly looking old and tired.

'Doctor Sinclair, you are very good to me and I'll do what you say. I've got Meg here and I'll be all right.'

Not long after Dr Sinclair had left and Meg had given Mrs Peacock her breakfast, Meg heard Mrs Coates answer the front door. It's not Geoffrey, she thought. He always walks straight in after ringing the bell and in any case, I can hear more than one voice.

Then an agitated voice was heard on the stairs. It was Mrs Coates.

'Miss Meg, it's the police. They want to see you.'

'Me?' Meg answered. 'Why me?'

'I don't know, but they look a bit grim.'

Meg ran down the stairs and saw Detective Sergeant Boyes and Detective Constable Woodleigh standing in the hall.

'Nurse Bowering, we wish to ask you some more questions. Can we go somewhere quiet?'

'Yes, of course,' she replied, trying to hide her nervousness. 'We can use the living-room. Mrs Peacock isn't getting up until this afternoon.'

'How is she now? Can she be told the truth of the matter?'

'Dr Sinclair has been to tell her this morning. It was a shock to her but he gave her a sedative and she is resting.'

'Very well.' Sergeant Boyes motioned her to sit down. 'I have to tell you that we have pursued our enquiries and I must ask you to come to the police station at Hexton for further questioning.'

Meg stared from the sturdy sergeant

to the tall policewoman. What did they mean? Why should they want to question her?

'Did you hear, Nurse Bowering?'

'Yes . . . yes,' she faltered. 'But I don't understand.'

'Evidence has been laid against you and it is necessary for you to help us with our enquiries. I also have to tell you that we shall leave two policemen here to search the house while we are away.'

'Search the house?' Meg was totally bewildered. 'But what for? What are you looking for? I had nothing to do with it and I don't want Mrs Peacock upset. She has been very ill, you know that.'

'Mrs Peacock will not be on her own while you are at the police station, will she?'

'No, of course not. Mrs Coates will be here,' Meg replied.

'Mrs Coates, the housekeeper?'

'Yes.'

'Well, kindly go and tell her that you

are coming with us.'

Meg stood up and thought her legs would give way. She couldn't begin to imagine where all this was leading.

The next few hours were one long nightmare for Meg but throughout, she somehow remembered Andrew telling her to be honest. She thought of him and took courage. They seemed to be at the Hexton Police Station in minutes and she was taken to a small, bare interview room where she sat at a table with a tape-recorder on it.

Sergeant Boyes gave her name and the date and the time and the questions started. They began with the usual warning that her words would be used in evidence and she felt frightened.

'Nurse Bowering, you know that Mrs Peacock was given arsenic in what we believe was an attempt to kill her?'

'Yes.'

'Do you know how the arsenic was administered?'

'The doctor at the hospital said that it was in her medicine.'

'What was the medicine for?'

'She was taking it for stomach pains believed to be caused by the drugs she was taking for her arthritis.'

'Who usually gave her the medicine?'

'I did.'

'How?'

'What do you mean?'

'Was it given by spoon?'

'Oh, no, it was in a small measuring cup and she drank it. It was not unpleasant.'

'Did anyone else have access to the medicine?'

'Well, only Mrs Coates and . . . '

A memory that had temporarily disappeared came flooding back.

'And . . . Nurse Bowering?'

Geoffrey, Geoffrey, she was thinking. You did it, didn't you? It's just as Mrs Peacock said, you did it for the money.

'I'm sorry, I can't say.'

'Then I'll ask you again, Nurse Bowering, did anyone else have access to the medicine?'

'Once, on a Friday afternoon, I was about to go into the living-room and I overheard a conversation between Mrs Peacock and her nephew. She was saying she had stomach pains and he said he would give her some of her medicine.'

'But on that occasion, she wasn't very ill afterwards?'

'She was uncomfortable but not very ill.'

Meg knew that she hadn't told the whole truth but something was holding her back. For some reason she couldn't explain, she seemed to be trying to shelter Geoffrey. She had no concrete evidence and it seemed almost impossible that Geoffrey could have committed such a dreadful crime.

'To go back to last Friday, when did you last see Geoffrey Peacock?'

'I saw him early in the afternoon. We had a disagreement, then he had tea with his aunt and when I came into the house I could hear them arguing.'

'You listened to what they said?'

'Yes.'

'What did you hear?'

'They were arguing about money.'

'And did Mrs Peacock mention her will?'

With a flash of insight, Meg realised that they had set a trap for her and she was entangled, unable to escape.

'Yes,' she said and almost felt herself tremble.

'Do you remember her words?'

'Mrs Peacock said she could change her will and not leave her fortune to Geoffrey. In fact, she had already changed it and . . .'

'And?'

It had to be said.

'She said she was going to leave me ten thousand pounds.'

'Is that a lot of money to you, Nurse Bowering?'

'Yes.'

'And was it enough for you to try to murder her for?'

Meg jumped up then.

'It's not true what you are saying. I

134

know it looks as though I had a motive but I didn't do it. It wasn't me! It was Geoffrey.'

The words were out! She had said it at last.

'You suspect that Geoffrey Peacock tried to murder his aunt?'

'Yes, I do and . . . '

'Wait a moment. Would it surprise you to know that Mr Peacock thought that you had given his aunt the poison and has laid charges against you?'

Things went black. The room went round and Meg felt the policewoman's hand on her arm, holding a cup of water to her lips. The sergeant's face came back into focus.

'What do you mean?' Meg stammered.

'I have to tell you that we have not been able to trace Mr Geoffrey Peacock. He is wanted for questioning because he benefits most from his aunt's death. The farm has been searched and on his desk in the office, we found a note addressed to the police. You can read it.'

He handed her a piece of paper but the words swam before Meg's eyes.

To the police — In the affair of the poisoning of Mrs Ethel Peacock, you need look no further than Melbeck House. You will find that Nurse Bowering had access to arsenic and regularly gave Mrs Peacock her medicine. Ask her if she would benefit from Mrs Peacock's will. She had the means, the motive and the opportunity and I think that you will find that you can charge her with attempted murder of my aunt.

Meg read it slowly and Geoffrey's words made her feel sick. She could remember his voice.

'I'll get even with you yet,' he had said and now things looked black against her.

She couldn't speak but at that moment, a uniformed policeman came into the room and handed a note to Sergeant Boyes who read it quickly.

'Nurse Bowering,' he said to Meg, 'it is as Mr Peacock said. You had the motive for murdering Mrs Peacock and now we know that you had the means. Arsenic has been found in your bedroom and I hereby charge you with . . . '

Meg heard no more. She thought she was going mad. She cried out, screaming.

'I didn't have any arsenic. I didn't do it even if Geoffrey says I did and you have the proof against me. It was Geoffrey. I know I can't prove it but it was Geoffrey who did it . . . why has he disappeared, tell me that . . . it was Geoffrey, I tell you, it was Geoffrey!'

'Nurse Bowering, you will be taken to a cell until you can arrange legal advice. Is there anyone who would help you?'

'Yes.' She sobbed. 'Yes, there is. Please get Andrew, he's the vicar of Nether Rawcliffe, Andrew Sheratt.'

It was a clean, small cell they took Meg to, not uncomfortable. She sat on the bunk and tried to calm down. A woman police constable brought her a cup of coffee and that helped. She could hardly believe what was happening but she knew that Geoffrey had said he would cause her trouble when she refused to marry him.

He must have planted the arsenic in her room. Where did they find it, she wondered. And surely it would have her fingerprints on it if she had touched it. They would find only his, she was sure. And yet they had brought her to this cell, accusing her of the crime seemingly just on the evidence of Geoffrey's word and the packet of arsenic.

She threw herself down and let herself cry, knowing she was innocent, knowing that Geoffrey was a wicked person but what power did she have to help herself? Then she felt a hand on her shoulder. Startled, she looked up to see a tall, dark figure. It was Andrew, and he had thoughtfully worn his cassock.

'Meg, Meg, whatever has happened? Why are you in a cell?'

She clung to him and tried to tell

him but was almost incoherent. He dragged the story from her, stroking her head but not saying anything. When it came to the words of Geoffrey's accusation, he got up suddenly.

'Meg, stay here. Try not to cry. Leave it to me.'

He left the cell and while he was gone, someone came in and took her fingerprints. In the meantime, Andrew had sought out Sergeant Boyes and they had a long talk. Andrew, knowing that he was betraying a confidence, told the sergeant all that Meg had told him of her suspicions of Geoffrey and of Geoffrey's threats to cause trouble for her and to get his own back.

Another report was brought to the sergeant and he gave his first smile, turning to Andrew at the same time.

'I think we have some good news, vicar. The prints on the packet of arsenic are not those of Nurse Bowering but match those of Mr Geoffrey Peacock that we have found at the farm. Thank you for your help. You can take her home now though you had better warn her that she will need to make another statement later on.'

Andrew didn't take Meg back to Melbeck House immediately but took her straight to a hotel and ordered coffee and some biscuits. Meg couldn't believe that it was not yet lunchtime. Andrew talked quietly to her in a reassuring voice and gradually her confidence returned.

When they arrived back at Melbeck House, it was to find pandemonium in the kitchen, with Mrs Coates crying and Mrs Manthorpe excitedly waving a book about. Meg ran in, followed by Andrew.

'Mrs Coates, whatever is the matter? I'm home!'

Mrs Coates threw her arms around her.

'Oh, Miss Meg, I think we've found the proof that it was Mr Geoffrey. Tell them, Ida.'

Mrs Manthorpe put the book on the kitchen table.

'Better not touch it any more,' she said. 'It might have fingerprints on it.'

'But what is it, Mrs Manthorpe?' Meg asked, then she bent over and read the title of the book which had a shiny new cover. ' 'Poisons And Their Uses,' ' she said and they were silent.

'I saw him reading it one day in his office and he covered it up when I came into the room and . . . well, somehow he looked guilty, a nasty kind of look on his face. Well, yesterday, the police searched the whole house. I suppose they were looking for the arsenic but they didn't find anything.

'After they'd gone, I got to thinking and remembered Mr Geoffrey and this book. So I went and looked but I couldn't find it anywhere, then this morning, I just thought I'd look in the big glass bookcase in the drawingroom and there it was. You'd never have noticed it if you weren't looking for it. Vicar, where are you going?'

'I'm going to phone Sergeant Boyes. I think he ought to know straight away.

It might be important.' He turned to Meg. 'Meg, I think you should go and see if Mrs Peacock is all right. Do you feel up to it?'

'Yes, of course I will, but don't go before I've seen you, Andrew.'

On the way home from Hexton, Andrew and Meg had decided to tell Mrs Peacock that Meg had gone to the police station simply to answer questions. She need not know about Geoffrey's accusation and the subsequent events, Andrew said, and Meg thankfully agreed.

Upstairs, Meg found a very cheerful and determined Mrs Peacock.

'Meg,' she cried out, 'you've come back. Will you let the police know that I want to see them, too? I'm quite well enough now. I've done a lot of thinking this morning and I've decided I'm not going to let Geoffrey get away with it. I'm all right, but it was a wicked thing to do and it must have been Geoffrey. There are only you and Mrs Coates in the house and the more I think of it, the more I believe that he has been giving me the stuff for some time. It was always after he'd gone that I had those pains. He probably wanted it to look as though I had something wrong with my stomach so that when he gave me the big dose, no-one would suspect and I'd be gone and he could just pocket the money.'

Meg couldn't help smiling. It was the first time that day.

'You may be right, Mrs Peacock, but we'll have to wait and see what the police come up with. You are all right now, that's the main thing.'

'I'm sorry about Geoffrey. I shouldn't be accusing my own nephew should I, but justice must be done. Would it mean prison, do you think?'

She's incorrigible, Meg thought, but I suppose she's right.

'Geoffrey's disappeared, Mrs Peacock, and Mrs Manthorpe has found a book of poisons at the farm so it looks as though you are right. Will you have some lunch now?'

'Yes, please, dear, and afterwards, I'll have a nap and then you can get me up.'

Meg went back downstairs to say goodbye to Andrew.

'The police are on their way,' he said. 'Can you cope? I think they'll want to see Mrs Peacock as well.'

'And she wants to see them! She's in good form, Andrew. I think that Geoffrey's been a thorn in her flesh for years and she'll be quite pleased if he's disappeared. She even asked if he'd have to go to prison!'

'Oh, dear,' Andrew said. 'And I used to think she was a nice old lady.' He laughed.

'She's a darling,' Meg said. 'And, Andrew, you're a darling, too. I don't know how to thank you.'

He put his hands on her shoulders and she looked up and met his smiling eyes.

'Perhaps I will let you thank me, one day,' he said softly and gave her a quick kiss. 'There is something I want to tell you but I don't think today is the day.'

He wants to tell me about Jill, Meg thought, as she waved goodbye. Perhaps they have agreed to get married at last. Her parting thoughts were sad and happy at the same time.

7

Meg didn't have time to grieve about the thought of Andrew and Jill getting married. The police were at Melbeck House within minutes, asking her to make another statement. She told the whole truth of it then, how she had listened at the door, how she had become suspicious when Mrs Peacock was worse after every Friday visit that Geoffrey made.

Then they saw Mrs Peacock. Meg stayed with her and was pleased at the gentle way Sergeant Boyes spoke to her. Mrs Peacock was her usual forthright self and confirmed all that Meg had said.

She said that, thinking back, it had all begun when he started putting her sugar in her tea for her, then she would get the pains and he would insist on giving her the medicine. No, she hadn't taken any notice when he poured it into the little measuring cup. She was used to Meg doing it for her and it usually helped her but on Fridays, it always made her worse. Now she knew why.

While Sergeant Boyes was at Melbeck House, a team of policemen were combing the farm and the sergeant was called from the room in the middle of the interview. When he came back, he went straight up to Meg and shook her by the hand.

'Nurse Bowering, it is good news for you. Traces of arsenic have been found in the pocket of Mr Peacock's jacket and an examination of the book on poisons has revealed that the pages devoted to arsenic poisoning are the only ones to show any signs of use or finger marks. We have a case against Mr Peacock. He had both motive and means.'

'But you've got to find him,' Mrs Peacock burst in.

'You are right, ma'am, but as he was last seen putting a large suit-case into

147

his car when Mrs Manthorpe thought he must be going to the hospital, it looks as though he might have given us the slip. It's very easy to get out of the country, a short trip to an airport, shuttle to Heathrow and you can go anywhere in the world as long as you know the places which have no extradition agreements with us. Bigger criminals than Mr Peacock have done the same quite successfully. We are powerless. Now I must ask you one more thing, Mrs Peacock. Did Mr Peacock have any close friends nearby, any relatives?'

'Carla Handley,' Mrs Peacock replied instantly. 'No relatives but he's been close to Carla Handley for years. I thought they would marry at one time but nothing came of it.'

'And she lives locally?'

'Yes, just out of the village, a big house on the road up the dale. She's a wealthy widow and I think she's fond of Geoffrey in her own way, but I never liked her.'

Sergeant Boyes got up.

'Well, you've both been very helpful and I'm pleased you've made a good recovery, ma'am. I don't think it will be necessary for us to come again but I know I can rely on your co-operation.'

For the remainder of the day, it was hard to settle down. Mrs Peacock had a rest, Meg phoned Andrew to tell him the latest news and then took a walk up on to the moor. After all that had happened in the last few days, it seemed absolute bliss to be on her own, out in the open, with the relief of knowing she wasn't going to be charged with attempted murder.

She thought about Geoffrey. He really is a wicked person, she said to herself and yet he was so attractive and could be very kind. I wouldn't like to see him in prison in spite of what Mrs Peacock says. Perhaps he has got away, but I wonder if we'll ever know.

Before the end of the afternoon, she had a phone call from Sergeant Boyes.

'Just to let you know that Mr

Peacock's Range Rover has been found at Leeds-Bradford Airport and Mrs Handley has been interviewed. He confessed everything to her and she has been very honest with us. I think she will be joining him wherever he is. We can't stop her. She seems to have known nothing of what was going on and it was quite a shock to her when he told her. I thought you would like to know and that you will tell Mrs Peacock.'

Meg went to have tea with Mrs Peacock and told her about the phone call.

'I suppose I'm pleased,' was Mrs Peacock's reaction. 'He deserves to be punished but I suppose he's made his own punishment getting out of the country and knowing that he can never come back without being brought to trial and sent to prison. Imagine having that hanging over you for the rest of your life.'

'What will you do about the farm, Mrs Peacock?'

'No question,' Mrs Peacock replied. 'I'll have Rory's son over. He's a farmer and I gather he's struggling in Ireland. I'll be glad to see him here if he'll come. In a way it will keep the farm in the family even if he's a McGuire and not a Peacock. You don't always get what you want in life, do you?'

Meg went away thinking of Mrs Peacock's last words. No, you don't always get what you want, she said to herself, but I suppose the only thing to do is to think of the happiness of other people as Mrs Peacock is doing about her cousins. That is important to her, Meg said to herself, and so must Andrew's happiness be important to me.

He phoned her that evening to make sure that she was all right and she thought it was kind of him. She told him the latest news and he was pleased that it had all ended well. He said very little about Geoffrey. No sooner had Meg replaced the receiver than she heard a knock at the front door and

Mrs Coates letting someone in. It was a female voice.

Meg went downstairs into the hall and was astonished to see Carla, looking quite different. Gone was the former air of superiority and Meg felt quite sorry for her.

'Meg, I've come to see you. Geoffrey asked me to. I must tell you that I've had a considerable shock and it's been a difficult week-end. But then it has been for you, too, and I'm glad it's all out in the open. I'm going away sometime tomorrow.'

'Are you going to join Geoffrey?' Meg asked.

'Yes.' Carla nodded. 'I'll tell you about it in a minute.'

Meg left Carla in the living-room and went to the kitchen to make some coffee. It was a warm evening but she thought that the coffee would give Carla a boost.

'I've got a lot to tell you,' Carla began. 'It's hard to know where to start.'

'Did you know what Geoffrey was up to?' Meg asked.

'No, I didn't, that's why it was such a shock when he told me what had happened. I knew he was in serious financial trouble with his wretched racing losses and that he had taken money from the farm's capital. I knew that his aunt wouldn't advance him the money and I refused, too. I wish I had given it to him now. I could have spared it.'

Carla looked at Meg.

'But as you know, I was feeling jealous and put out because he was paying attention to you and I didn't feel like settling his gambling debts. But I'd no idea he'd go to such awful lengths. Geoffrey has always been such a kind person. He's been a good friend to me for many years and I've never discovered any wicked streak in him. I think it was the desperation about the money that drove him to it.'

'When did you find out, Carla?'

'It was first thing on Saturday

morning. I was having a late breakfast when he suddenly arrived on my doorstep. He said he had a lot to tell me. It was such a terrible shock, Meg. He said the police would be looking for him because his aunt had been poisoned and was in hospital. Then he said, I'm sorry Meg, he said that he had deliberately incriminated you and that the police would arrest you for attempted murder. Is that what happened, Meg?'

'Yes,' Meg replied. 'He left the police a note.'

'But why, Meg, why did he want you to take the blame for it? I thought he liked you.'

'It was easy, Carla. I refused to marry him. He knew that if I became engaged to him and that Mrs Peacock thought he was going to settle at the farm with me then she would give him the money. But I refused.'

'Why did you refuse? I thought you found him attractive.'

Meg laughed.

'Oh, he was attractive enough, I don't deny that, but I never took to him and in any case, I loved someone else.'

'But it was such a dreadful thing to do to let the suspicion rest on you. It was bad enough what he'd done in any case without trying to put the blame on you.'

Meg remembered something and was curious.

'Carla, did he tell you when he put the arsenic in my room. Had it been there a long time?'

'No, I don't think he ever meant you to be accused. He had got it all carefully planned. He had given his aunt a little arsenic each week in her tea and in her medicine to make it look as though she'd an ulcer or something. Then I think he intended to increase the dose so that when she died it would look like natural causes and he would get away with it.'

Carla gave a shudder.

'Oh, it was such a terrible, cold-blooded thing to do to an old lady like Mrs Peacock. I think he must have been out of his mind with the worry about the money.'

'But it didn't work out as he had planned,' Meg persisted.

'No. Although he'd started giving his aunt the poison, he was still hoping you would agree to marry him and everything would be all right. But after he had seen you that afternoon and you had said no again, he rushed back into the house in a temper and before he went to see Mrs Peacock, he slipped up to your bedroom and hid the arsenic packet.'

Meg interrupted.

'But he gave her a bigger dose a few minutes later.'

'Yes, I realise that. He'd emptied some powder from the packet into his pocket.'

'Oh, that explains it.'

'Explains what?' Carla asked.

'The police found traces of arsenic in

one of his jackets. That was what finally nailed him and took the suspicion away from me.'

'I think criminals are always careless somewhere along the line. They make a slip somewhere and that's what finds them out in the end. And whatever else we might think of Geoffrey, it was a criminal thing to do.'

Carla was silent for a few moments and Meg wondered if she had heard the end of the story but Carla continued to speak.

'I think he was sorry at what he'd done as soon as he realised that his aunt had been taken to hospital. He didn't sleep much that night planning what he was going to do.'

'But he left that note for the police about me.'

'I'm sorry, Meg, and I think Geoffrey was sorry. After he'd told me the whole story, he said he'd done an even worse thing, left a note for the police to tell them you did it. He meant to destroy it but in the rush to get away, he forgot and was still on his desk. I tried to persuade him to go back and destroy it even if he meant to evade justice himself but he was dashing to the airport and hadn't left enough time. So he told me to tell you he was sorry and he was sure everything would be all right in the end.'

'But he didn't know if Mrs Peacock was alive or dead.'

'Yes, he did. He made me ring the hospital while he was here, so I did and I was told she'd had a comfortable night and was much stronger. So he went then.'

'But, Carla, you've left it all that time to come forward. You could have saved us all the trouble we've been in and me going to the police station and everything. Why didn't you come forward sooner?'

'I promised Geoffrey I wouldn't do anything for forty-eight hours while he got away. I was just about to go to the police when they came to me. That's all, Meg, you know it all now. I can only say I'm sorry for everything.'

'Well, you did come and see me, Carla. I appreciate that. What are you going to do now?'

'I've spent the whole week-end putting the house in order. It's going on the market as it stands, furniture and everything. I'm flying to join Geoffrey tomorrow.'

'How can you, Carla?' Meg asked quietly, unable to understand.

'I love him, Meg. I have loved him for ten years. If I'd been able to have children, he'd have married me a long time ago. I think he's sorry for what he did. It wasn't the Geoffrey I've known and loved and I've a feeling he's learned a lesson from it. I have enough money for both of us but I shan't let him gamble it away. He's still young and we can buy a farm or he can manage an estate or something.'

Carla stood up and held out her hand to Meg.

'I know he has done wrong, Meg, but it doesn't stop me loving him.

I'll go now and leave you to think about what I've said but I hope that one day you'll find it in your heart to forgive him.'

Meg shook hands.

'I'll have to, Carla. Mrs Peacock hasn't come to any harm fortunately and that's what matters most to me. I wish you all the best and Geoffrey, too.'

'That's very generous of you, Meg, and I shall tell Geoffrey so. Goodbye.'

Meg saw Carla off, went up to see Mrs Peacock who was reading in bed and told her some of the things that Carla had said.

'If you think back, Meg, I suppose I was partly to blame,' Mrs Peacock said surprisingly.

Meg looked at her in astonishment.

'If I hadn't been so insistent that we must have a Peacock heir for High Aiskew, Geoffrey would probably have married Carla years ago and I believe she would have been a good wife to him and kept him straight. But it didn't work out that way and it has caused a lot of trouble. However, I've survived and I can only hope that Geoffrey makes up for his wickedness by making a good life somewhere in the world with Carla. I don't suppose we shall ever see either of them again.'

Meg could hardly sleep that night. The events of that day were whirling and reeling in her mind until she began to wonder if it had all really happened. She must look to the future now, a future without Geoffrey, a future without Andrew and an immediate future which would lead to the coming of the McGuire family to High Aiskew Farm.

The rest of that month slipped by and life resumed its normal pattern. Meg saw Andrew occasionally and she met Jill once a week. The two of them were busy planning the first aid class for the Youth Club which was due to re-open at the beginning of September.

Meg was looking forward to the start

of the classes and had got all the equipment she needed bought with the funds which Andrew had provided from the Youth Club account.

On the first evening, Mrs Peacock had agreed to go to bed early so that Meg could get down to the club in plenty of time. Hers was the only car in the village hall carpark so it surprised her when she entered the hall to hear laughter and an excited female voice.

She stopped in the doorway. In the middle of the empty hall stood Andrew and Jill. He had his arms round her and was kissing her.

Meg turned and ran back to the car. They hadn't seen her and she didn't want them to see how upset she was. Although she had been expecting it, the sight of them in each other's arms had come as a shock. They must have just got engaged, she was saying to herself. They both looked so happy. I must be happy for them, too. She wiped away a tear, took a deep breath, got her things together again and went back to the hall.

By this time, Andrew was standing by the door, looking very pleased.

'Meg, I was just coming to look for you. I thought I heard a car. We've got some great news.'

Jill came up rather shyly and Meg looked from one of them to the other.

'You've got engaged,' she said. 'Congratulations.'

Two pairs of eyes looked at her in amazement and both Andrew and Jill burst out laughing. Andrew took Meg's arm and drew her into the hall.

'No, Meg, no,' he was saying. 'You've got it wrong. We're not engaged. It's Jill you've got to congratulate.'

But Meg didn't understand and she looked at Jill who went up to her and kissed her.

'Meg, I couldn't tell you before. I've got engaged to David. It's David I'm going to marry.'

'David Courtney?'

'Yes, that's right,' Jill replied.

'But I'd no idea, you never said anything. I thought you were just good friends.'

Jill smiled.

'It's a long story and I can't tell you now. The children will soon be here. When club is finished, come for a walk with me and I'll tell you all about it. Are you pleased?'

Meg gave her a kiss.

'Very, very pleased and I can't wait to hear all about it.'

The first aid class went very well. The young people were keen and interested and it made a good start to the evening. After a break for tea and biscuits, they had their usual table tennis and darts or danced and listened to music.

Andrew left halfway through the evening and Meg scarcely had a chance to speak to him or to ask him if he was pleased at Jill's news.

'Meg,' he said. 'I can't stop now. I've got an old lady to visit, who had a fall this afternoon. Come for a walk with me on Saturday when I come and see Mrs Peacock.'

Meg promised gladly and watched him go. She had no way of telling if he was upset at losing Jill to David but he hadn't seemed heartbroken. Perhaps he was putting a brave face on it for Jill's sake, Meg thought.

They locked up the hall and as it was a fine evening and not yet dark, Meg and Jill decided to walk down to the river. They chatted all the way about the evening and then when they were standing by the side of the river looking at the clear water bubbling over the stones, Meg at last put her question.

'Well, Jill Burnett, are you going to tell me or not! Was David the one you told me about? You said you were in love with someone but he didn't love you. I thought it must be Andrew.'

'No. I'm very fond of Andrew. He's always been a good friend but I never loved him in that way though I think half the village thought I did.'

Meg laughed.

'It was one of the first things I learned from Mrs Peacock. You've been very secretive. However have you managed to keep it a secret all this time?'

Jill was serious with a somewhat sad look in her eyes.

'Well, you see, it's only a year since David's wife died. It was a terrible tragedy and David was left with the two little girls. He got an au pair but I got into the habit of going in to help him when it was the au pair's day off. He was grateful and we became good friends. We had always got on very well at school.'

She stopped, dreamy-eyed and thoughtful.

'But I fell in love with him. I thought it was awful falling in love with a man so recently bereaved but I just couldn't help myself. He didn't know, as I hid my feelings the best I could and I didn't tell a soul, not even you or Andrew. It was something I had to keep to myself.'

'And all the time, he was falling in love with you,' Meg said.

'Well, not at first. He was still grieving for Sally, but we've had some happy times with the girls this summer. You saw us when we took them iceskating in Leeds. Then last night, well this sounds silly but it's funny really and rather marvellous. I was round at his house and the girls were in bed and I was making coffee in the kitchen. I accidentally spilled some water and slipped on the wet floor. David helped me up and I was in his arms, and, well, that was it.

'He admitted that he loved me. He couldn't believe it for it was quite different to how he felt for Sally and would I marry him though not for a little while. So we've got engaged and we're going to buy a ring on Saturday. The girls are so excited.'

Jill's eyes were shining and Meg gave her a quick hug.

'I couldn't be more pleased,' she said. 'I've only met David twice but he seems really nice and you'll have the school in common. I do wish you every happiness, Jill. It's the best news I've heard for a long time.'

They strolled back to the hall across the darkening fields. Both were busy with their own thoughts, Jill thinking of her good fortune in finding David and Meg wondering about Andrew's feelings at losing Jill.

8

The days got shorter and the mornings colder and crisper as September crept towards October but Meg was to find she saw very little of Andrew. They had walked up on to the moor on the afternoon he came up to see Mrs Peacock and she had enjoyed his company even though they had only talked of the events surrounding Mrs Peacock's illness and Geoffrey's disappearance.

She had the feeling that he seemed to think that she must be missing Geoffrey a lot and she didn't quite know how to say that she was glad she was never going to see him again.

After that, she didn't see much of him and found that she was very disappointed, at the same time not being sure what she had expected after the announcement of Jill's

169

engagement to David.

On Youth Club nights, she always seemed to have the hope that he would ask her to go for a drink afterwards or even for a walk though this was unlikely as the darker evenings approached. But he left the club halfway through each evening just as he had always done.

Then, out of the blue, Mrs Peacock started to ask him to lunch on a Saturday. On one of his visits, he had admitted that he didn't cook a lot at week-ends and that for him, Sunday was a sandwich day. Mrs Peacock knew she couldn't invite him to lunch on Sundays so Saturday was settled upon and soon became rather a nice habit which Meg found herself looking forward to.

Late in September, the McGuire family arrived at the farm and Meg took Andrew down to introduce them to him. That day, Meg and Andrew took the long path round the back of the farm that led up to the moor and back to Melbeck House from the opposite direction to the one that Meg was used to taking.

They talked about the McGuires as they walked along.

'I think Mrs Peacock will be happier with her cousins running the farm. She was never happy about Geoffrey, was she?' He gave Meg a sudden keen look. 'Do you miss him, Meg?'

Meg looked astonished. He had hinted at this before but had never asked her a direct question.

'Miss Geoffrey Peacock? Me? You must be joking.'

'I thought you were quite keen on him at one time. You often met him up on the moor, didn't you?'

'Andrew Sheratt, you've been listening to village gossip. I'm ashamed of you!'

She felt cross but she tried not to show it but then she wondered if it had bothered Andrew that she had met Geoffrey on the moor.

'If you must know, he used to ride up from the farm and join me on Melbeck Moor just at the time that

I'd gone for a nice, quiet walk to be on my own. I can assure you, he was never welcome. And then all that business started about marrying him and you know how that ended up for I told you all about it.'

'You would have been a wealthy farmer's wife by now if you had married him,' was his next remark and Meg found it hard to imagine what was in his mind.

'Andrew, a farmer's wife is the last thing I would want to be even in a lovely old farmhouse like High Aiskew and you should know me well enough by now to know that being very wealthy isn't one of the more important ambitions of my life. And I didn't love Geoffrey, in any case. I would never marry without love.'

'Wouldn't you, Meg? Is that important to you?'

'Very important,' she said firmly.

'I'm glad to hear you say that,' he replied and abruptly changed the subject and started talking of other things all the way home, leaving Meg to think that he must still be broken-hearted about Jill turning to David Courtney.

When they reached Melbeck House, Andrew said goodbye and thank you to Mrs Peacock who said she looked forward to seeing him again next week. Meg watched him go almost in despair, her heart aching to think of him and she told herself that she must forget love and be content to have him for a friend.

On Monday, Meg was in her room preparing for her usual afternoon walk when Mrs Coates came hurrying up the stairs and tapped on the door.

'Miss Meg, are you thinking of going for your walk? Oh, you are just getting ready.'

Meg always changed from her uniform into denims and an anorak to go out walking and Mrs Coates could see that she was nearly ready.

'The sky doesn't look too good from the kitchen window, Miss Meg. I think the cloud is going to come down. You don't want to be caught up on the moor if the cloud is down. You'd never find your way back. Were you going to your usual place?'

Meg was looking out of the window. It wasn't a bright, fine day but the cloud was broken and her unpractised eye could see no sign of a deterioration in the weather. She turned to look at the worried housekeeper.

'I shan't be gone long, Mrs Coates, just up to the stones and back. I know it so well by now that I'm sure I could find my way even in a mist.'

'Well, you take care and if it comes down, you're to stay where you are until it clears. That's the rule, Miss Meg. You could easily get lost.'

'I'll be all right, Mrs Coates. Don't you start worrying about me.'

Meg set off cheerfully. Often it was the only exercise she got during the day and her only chance of leaving the house. She looked forward to the walk and always enjoyed it.

She took her time climbing up the steep path to the top then set off at a brisk pace until she reached the stones. Here she always stopped to have a rest and today was no exception though she was rather surprised and alarmed to find that the opposite side of the dale was completely blotted out, almost as though it wasn't there.

I hope Mrs Coates wasn't right, she said to herself. I'd better not linger too long. But she started to think about Andrew as she usually did and soon lost track of time. He had asked her some strange and pointed questions on Saturday. Surely he didn't really think that she had cared for Geoffrey?

And all the time, it seemed as though he was on the brink of telling her something then he stopped, stalled. It had happened more than once. She loved him as much as ever but she could hardly blurt out her love especially when she had no idea what his feelings were about Jill.

She had settled down again after

the turmoil and upset of Geoffrey's behaviour. She loved her job and she was very fond of Mrs Peacock. She also loved Wedderdale and belonging to a small community. Her one little ache of unhappiness was her unrequited love for Andrew.

Meg, engrossed in her thoughts, hadn't noticed that the cloud was coming down but she suddenly felt chilled and thought it was time to be returning. It was misty at the stones which were in a sheltered dip in the hill and as she moved up to the path, it was as though she had walked into a thick blanket of very wet fog.

She stopped, alarmed. She couldn't see the path, and in those seconds, she seemed to have lost all sense of direction. She managed to grope her way back to the stones, tripping over tussocks of heather. She was thankful when she felt the cold stone, now completely engulfed in the cloud.

Now I've done it, Meg thought. I shouldn't have stayed so long. Mrs

Coates was right. She told me I mustn't move and I can now see why. She sat in a corner between two stones hoping to get some shelter from the penetrating wetness of the cloud.

She took a scarf out of her pocket and put it on and then put her hood up. That made her feel better. She was also pleased to discover that she'd a packet of mints in the depths of her pocket. She had no idea how long the cloud could hang about on the moor and although it was still early in the afternoon, it was October, and the evenings were drawing in.

Back at Melbeck House, Mrs Coates was keeping an anxious eye on the moor. She hadn't lived in Wedderdale for nearly sixty years for nothing. When she saw the top disappear and Meg hadn't returned, she hurried in to Mrs Peacock who was just waking up from her sleep.

'Mrs Peacock, ma'am, I'm right worried. Miss Meg has gone up to the stones and the cloud has come down. I did warn her but she would insist on going.'

Mrs Peacock was immediately alert and quick to think.

'Phone Andrew, and see if he can come. Tell him Meg is lost on the moor and he'll need a strong torch because the cloud is down.'

'But she's not really lost. I told her to stay put.'

'Do as I say and don't lose any time. He'll be up here in ten minutes if you can manage to catch him in.'

Andrew was in and didn't lose any time just as Mrs Peacock had said. He came in and spoke to them briefly making sure that Meg had gone up the usual path.

For the first few hundred yards, up the steepest part, it was still clear and he made the moor in no time then set off in the direction of the stones. Then, as Meg had found before him, he was enveloped in a blanket of cloud and was almost stopped in his tracks. He used the torch carefully to pick out the path and managed to keep to it, not straying on to the rough heather.

Then he started to call Meg's name not knowing where he would find her but hoping that she'd had the sense to stay at the stones, also hoping that he was going the right way and hadn't lost his sense of direction.

Meg thought she heard a voice calling out, then there was silence and she knew she had started to imagine things. But a few seconds later, the sound came again and she jumped up. The call had sounded like her name.

'I'm here,' she yelled back. 'Whoever you are, I'm here. I'm here.'

'Meg.'

It couldn't possibly be Andrew!

'Meg.'

'I'm here, by the stones,' she called back into the gloom.

Then she saw the gleam of the torch, heard the steps on the path.

'Meg, it's Andrew.'

'Oh, Andrew.'

He reached the stones and Meg threw

herself into his arms. Still clutching the torch, he held her close. Her cold, wet cheeks were against his and Andrew sought for her lips. They had kissed before and surprised each other but this time there was no surprise. It was a homecoming.

At last she pulled away, caught her breath and whispered his name. He drew her beside him to sit on the nearest stone, his arms still close around her, his cheek against hers.

'Andrew, how did you . . . '

He stopped her with another kiss.

'Explanations afterwards. Nothing is going to stop me telling you what I've wanted to tell you for so long. Meg, I love you so much. Please tell me that you love me, too.'

Meg couldn't believe that she had heard the words correctly.

'You love me, Andrew?' she asked tremulously.

'I love you, Meg. I have loved you for a long, long time but I dared not tell you, things kept getting in the way.'

He found her lips again in a sweet, gentle kiss, full of the love he had just declared.

'But you, Meg, can you possibly love me? Was your kiss telling me the truth?'

Meg said it then, the words she had been longing to say to him.

'I love you, too, Andrew.'

She almost cried then but they ended up laughing, hugging and kissing each other.

'How did you know where I was, Andrew? I can't believe that you are here.'

'Mrs Coates phoned me to tell me you were lost on the moor, that the cloud had come down and I was to bring a strong torch, as Mrs Peacock said so.'

'Oh, the dears,' Meg said and they laughed again. 'But I wasn't really lost. They shouldn't have alarmed you. I thought I was going to be here all night and I'd only got half a packet of mints and I was cold as well.'

'I'll keep you warm,' Andrew said. 'We'd better not move till it clears though I did manage to keep to the path with the help of the torch. I've got some chocolate in my pocket. I slipped it in just as I was leaving.'

'You're a darling.' She reached up and kissed his cheek. 'Andrew, why didn't you tell me before that you loved me? I thought you were still thinking about Jill, and upset when she got engaged to David.'

'I was very pleased for Jill. I'd guessed what was going on even though she'd tried to keep it to herself. We were always very good friends, Jill and I, but nothing more.'

'It's not what everyone thought,' she said.

Andrew grinned.

'I know, village gossip, but you get used to it after a while and take no notice. Meg, I've wanted to ask you but couldn't pluck up courage before. Will you marry me?'

Meg gave a glorious, happy smile.

'Yes, Andrew, I would love to marry you. I fell in love with you that day we went to Wedder Head. Come to think of it, we were soaking wet then. We aren't very romantic, are we? But tell me, Andrew, what were the things that got in the way?'

He looked at her seriously.

'I think I loved you from the first moment I met you but you were attracted to Geoffrey . . . no, don't interrupt. I know I was wrong now but I wasn't to know how you felt then. He was very attractive and was going to be very wealthy one day so I thought of him as being quite a catch. Then all those dreadful things happened and I had to give you time to get over them and, last of all, I simply got cold feet.'

'But why, Andrew, why?'

'We have to be serious, Meg. My stipend is very small. I can offer you a lovely house but hardly any money to keep it up. I just didn't think it was fair to ask you to share such a frugal life.'

'Oh, Andrew, money doesn't matter. In any case, I can go on nursing until . . . ' She broke off, embarrassed.

'Until we have a family,' he finished for her. 'You'd like a family, Meg?'

'Yes, please, I would,' she said emphatically and they kissed again then and Meg felt a dreamy contentment. Then she heard Andrew's voice again.

'Meg, have you noticed something?' She opened her eyes. 'The cloud has lifted.'

They had been so engrossed in themselves that they hadn't noticed that it was clear all round them and that they could see the other side of the dale.

'Oh, Andrew, it's beautiful. Will I really be making my home here?'

'You like the dale, Meg? You don't find it too isolated?'

She shook her head.

'No, I've had this feeling that it's where I'm meant to be and now I really do know why. Will you have to move one day, Andrew?'

'It's possible if I wanted promotion in

a bigger parish but I'm very contented here at the moment and even more so now that I've found you.'

She looked at him.

'Do you think we'd better go back? Mrs Peacock will want to know you've found me and I think that she's going to be pleased with our news.'

They hurried down the path and then ran the last hundred yards through the fields, arriving quite breathless at the garden gate where Andrew stopped.

'One more kiss before we go in. I love you, Meg.'

'And I love you, Andrew.'

They took off their wet anoraks in the kitchen and Mrs Coates quickly made tea and carried it through to the living-room. Mrs Peacock's eyes were bright and mischievous as she looked at them.

'Well, have you got any news for me?'

Meg went up to her and gave her a kiss on the cheek.

'Andrew has asked me to marry him

and I've said yes, Mrs Peacock.'

'About time, too,' she replied. 'I'm very pleased for both of you and hope you'll be very happy together.'

'What made you phone for Andrew?' Meg asked all of a sudden.

Mrs Peacock smiled.

'I had to get you together somehow,' she replied.

None of them could stop laughing and Mrs Peacock had almost the last word.

'I'd been inviting Andrew to lunch all this time and that didn't work so I hoped that being lost in the clouds might produce a romantic situation, and you see I was right. I suppose it means I shall lose you but I'm used to my nurses changing and at least I shall have the two of you nearby. Will you like living at the vicarage, Meg?' she asked.

Meg took hold of Andrew's hand and smiled up at him.

'I don't mind where I live as long as I'm with Andrew,' she said.